EARTH'S ELF

EARTH'S MAGIC BOOK 3

EVE LANGLAIS

Copyright © 2022 Eve Langlais

Cover by Addictive Covers © 2022

Produced in Canada

Published by Eve Langlais

http://www.EveLanglais.com

Canadian Intellectual Property Office Registration Number : 1191821

E-ISBN: 978 177 384 333 9

Print ISBN: 978 177 384 334 6

ALL RIGHTS RESERVED

This book is a work of fiction and the characters, events and dialogue found within the story are of the author's imagination and are not to be construed as real. Any resemblance to actual events or persons, either living or deceased, is completely coincidental.

No part of this book may be reproduced or shared in any form or by any means, electronic or mechanical, including but not limited to digital copying, file sharing, audio recording, email and printing without permission in writing from the author.

PROLOGUE

THE SOUTH POLE. T-MINUS TWELVE DAYS BEFORE CHRISTMAS.

"Did you hear something?" Paisleigh asked Maurice, the other guard working the overnight shift with her.

Maurice sucked on a candy cane, his booted feet on the desk, phone propped in his lap, watching something he must have downloaded since they didn't get any cellular signal this deep inside the glacier. The nights were long without some form of entertainment. She preferred to read.

"Probably just the bears going at it again." Maurice waggled his brows, and she grimaced at the reminder of the pair of males outside the icy facility that kept trying to catch the attention of the lone female in the area.

"I guess." She chewed her lower lip and tried to sink back into her story, only to slap the book shut as the hairs on her nape lifted. A nagging unease forced her to her feet as she tried to discern the source of her discomfort.

Scritch.

Faint but unmistakable.

This time Maurice heard it, too, and frowned as he set aside his phone. "Hunh. That's weird."

"It almost sounds as if it came from inside the containment area." She glanced at the heavily magicked bars over the deep shaft they guarded. An impenetrable prison for a heinous being. Not that Paisleigh had ever met or seen the prisoner. He'd been long locked away by the time she took her turn on guard rotation. Less guard and more a token presence to provide a warning system in the off chance the security holding one of the world's most dangerous entities had a flaw.

"Maybe it's a rat?" A less-than-certain suggestion from Maurice, who ignored the fact they'd never seen signs of any. The South Pole wasn't known for its rodent population.

"Should we check?"

Maurice thumped his feet to the ground. "Check how?"

Rather than reply, Paisleigh stood on the edge of the ice-limned grate, peering down, seeing nothing but darkness. Was their prisoner even still alive? She assumed those in charge knew; after all, they randomly dropped sacks with food inside. But then again, they never descended to check either.

"Not sure what you think you'll see," Maurice declared, joining her. "It's not like the prisoner can climb. The pit walls are smooth ice."

"What if he's managed to fashion himself some ice picks?"

"How? Nothing sent down can be used as a toothpick, let alone something durable enough to dig into the hard surface."

"But what if he did find a way?"

Her insistence caused Maurice to snort. "Let's say he did manage to make it to the top. The grate's not going anywhere. It's locked. The key is being kept safe in the North Pole, not to mention there are layers of magic. See?" He knelt down and brought his hand close enough to cause the protective layer to glow.

Groan.

This time the noise didn't come from the pit but overhead. They both craned to eye the icy ceiling. The glacier encasing the prison pit went a good hundred feet over them and was three times as wide. Only a single access tunnel allowed entry, and that only after being screened by the second set of guards outside. A set of six mages also rotated, checking on the wards, bringing supplies to the prisoner.

"You can't tell me that noise was normal," Paisleigh exclaimed.

"It is odd. Maybe we should check in with Helga and Bjorn." The guards at the entrance to the tunnel.

Paisleigh almost said, "Don't leave me," even as she couldn't have said why the sudden intense fear.

Maurice read her expression and did his best to reassure. "Don't look so worried. Most likely it's just climate change causing some cracking in the ice."

"What if it destabilizes the prison?" she squeaked.

"It can't. Not while the magic is intact." Those who'd

created the prison had accounted for all kinds of possibilities, including the glacier fracturing. "He ain't getting out."

She sure hoped not, because the whole reason why *he* had been locked away for all time was because of the danger he posed.

Creak.

They both eyed the ceiling, which remained whole. Still...

"Go. See what's happening." Paisleigh waved her hand at Maurice. "I'll be fine."

"You don't look fine. Tell you what. I'll stay here, and you go talk to our pals by the entrance. Reassure yourself."

"Are you sure?" She nibbled her lower lip.

"Totally sure. Ain't nothing to be afraid of. You'll see."

Maurice would know. He'd been working as a guard here for years compared to her three months. Yet, in all that time, not once had she heard any noises. Never had the hair on her nape lifted and given her a shiver. However, she'd heard the stories shared by the other guards. Rumors of those who'd gone missing. The voices some claimed they heard when no one was around.

She eyed the grate in the floor, hugged herself as a shudder hit her hard, and said, "I'll be quick." She'd head outside, see there was nothing to worry about, and return.

"Bring back some hot cocoa, would you? With

marshmallows," Maurice yelled as she headed into the icy tunnel bored into the glacier.

The chill of their location hit her as she left the warmth of the chamber heated with special stones that somehow didn't melt the ice. She scurried quickly, the only sound the huff of her breath. The scuff of her boots. The jingle of a bell—

Er, what?

She halted and listened.

Nothing. She glanced back and saw only the smooth, icy walls of the tunnel. Must have imagined it. She walked more slowly and heard it again.

Jingle.

Jangle.

Definitely a bell. Impossible. Bells weren't allowed in the pit chamber. Or anywhere else in the South Pole for that matter. Something about upsetting the magical shields of the prison.

Hesitating, she glanced back and then forward. Which way should she go?

The waft of cold air hinting of cinnamon from the direction of the pit decided her. Terrified, she ran full out, arms pumping, aiming for the hint of daylight at the end of the corridor.

At first, she thought it was her rapid gait making her unsteady, only to realize the ground underfoot shook. She braced her hand on the wall and felt it vibrating, humming against her palm.

Oh dear.

Not good.

Not good at all.

But even more worrisome was the sudden zigzagging crack that appeared overhead. Paisleigh bolted, struggling to keep her balance as the very floor buckled and heaved as ice groaned and cracked.

Impossible. The magic was supposed to prevent this from happening.

The rumbling intensified, and she lost her balance, hitting the floor on her knees. But that wasn't the worse of it. The sound of the ringing bell deepened.

JINGLE.

JANGLE.

"HO.

"HO.

"HO."

As an impossible voice resonated, the tunnel came down on top of Paisleigh.

She regained consciousness when the rescue crew dug her out of the icy rubble. Disoriented, she nonetheless gasped as she saw what remained of the glacier.

Nothing but ice chunks scattered all over.

But most terrifying of all was the realization of what had happened.

"The Earth mother help us all."

Santa had escaped.

CHAPTER
ONE

ANCHORAGE, ALASKA. PASSING THE TIME
READING A DROPPED FLYER.

DRINK UP, GRINCHES! HALF-PRICE LAP DANCES FOR EVERY pitcher you buy....

An expensive pitcher of lager, Leif would wager, tossing the flyer as he waited in a dirty alley outside a strip club. The neon lights at the front didn't penetrate the shadows as he waited for his target to emerge. He'd already peeked inside to confirm the tip and vetoed acting in public. The dim lighting and drunken patrons added too many unpredictable elements.

The alley provided the perfect spot to watch. Those leaving the club via the front had to cross the mouth of it to grab a taxi, as there was no stopping in front. If his target chose the more discreet exit into the alley itself, then even better.

As the witching hour neared, the club emptied, disgorging staggering drunks loudly speaking and gesturing to their companions. Silent patrons emerged, shoulders hunched as if not wanting to be noticed. It wasn't just men. A third of the audience now comprised women. Then there were the employees, waitresses and dancers alike, bodies and spirits tired after hours of smiling and being "on" for their audience. They moved quickly passed, covered neck to toe against the cold, hands in pockets. He'd wager more than a few clutched keys or sharp objects for the over-eager patron who needed a reminder the fantasy inside the bar didn't extend outside.

The people leaving slowed to a trickle, and still Leif hadn't seen his target. Had he been given the slip?

A high-pitched giggle, adorably sweet, raised the hair on his neck and indicated the end of his wait.

A long bare leg, finished in a stiletto heel, appeared first, the thighs barely covered by the sequined mini skirt, the fishnet stockings no protection against the cold. A short faux-fur jacket was the only semblance of warmth on the young woman passing by the alley. On her shoulder, an eight-inch cookie with a round head, two arms, two legs, iced with a bowtie and bright red buttons that matched its mouth.

A gingerbread man who'd come to life and, if left unchecked, a nuisance to society, pulling pranks, peeping, corrupting other food. It was Leif's job to apprehend him.

The stripper stopped at the mouth of the alley. But on the orders of her passenger.

Round black spots for eyes focused on Leif suddenly, spotting him amidst the shadows. The mouth twisted, and the brows shot down in an angry slant. "If it isn't one the North Pole's annoying soldiers."

Leif stepped into the middle of the alley, hands by his sides. "Don't make this harder than it has to be, Ralph." The target's real name. Ralph The Five Thousandth, to be exact. Those that came before having had unfortunate accidents. Living cookies had a short shelf life, and the gingers tended to be especially spicey about it.

"Why do you have to be such a narc, Leif? What's the harm in me having a little fun?" The gingerbread man eyed the stripper holding him and cooed, "Tell him, honey, you want to lick my icing."

"Depends, are the ingredients vegan?" queried the woman.

"Vegan!" huffed Ralph. "What is wrong with people these days? Trying to ruin a recipe that's lasted millennia." The cookie leapt from her shoulder, springing to the ground, and landing in a flourish with arms out swept.

"I don't put animals in my mouth." The woman strutted off, and Ralph managed a rude gesture that took both his arms before turning his attention to Leif. "Thanks a lot for ruining my night."

"Not my fault you're made with butter and eggs." Leif pulled out some ribbon. "Shall we get this over with?"

"What if I don't want to go back to Santa's Village? All everyone does is work, work, work."

Ironic coming from Ralph since he'd only ever played pranks. "You know the rules. Living cookies aren't allowed outside of the village." Because the non-magically inclined tended to get weird about their food talking back to them.

"So unfair." Ralph moped.

"You do realize they didn't send me after you until we got reports of you causing trouble."

"People these days can't take a joke."

"You hid inside a coffee shop and screamed, 'You're murdering my cousin,' every time someone ate a donut."

"I stand with my cake brothers."

"You can stand with them back at the village. Let's go."

A single brow arched, and the mouth rounded in mirth as Ralph giggled. "Only if you catch me." The cookie took off running.

Despite having expected this, Leif sighed. Why did the gingers always force them to chase? Probably because some of them actually did manage to escape. But Ralph had forgotten something. Leif wasn't just any soldier. Half elf from his father's side, half reindeer shifter from his mother. And not your run-of-the-mill forest buck. As a descendent of Santa's original sled team, Leif could fly.

He launched himself into the air and ran, his legs moving as if he were on the ground, only he moved above it, able to see Ralph and the many turns he took. Eventually, the cookie ran out of sugar and slowed.

Now was Leif's chance. He landed with a soft thud in front of Ralph, who backpedaled too slowly.

Leif grabbed hold of the squirmy cookie that yelled, "Let me go. I'm not going back."

"You need to stand and answer for your crimes." Ralph didn't just have a thing for strippers and making non-cryptids uncomfortable. In the short time since he came alive, he'd also smuggled drugs into the North Pole. The kind that had good people wandering into the ice fields outside their town shields, where they sometimes got eaten by a hungry polar or fell into a crevasse too deep to survive.

"Come on, Leif. You know what they'll do to me if you take me back," Ralph whined. "I'm too young to be eaten."

"We both know you're long past your best before-date."

"That's just a general guideline. Look at me." Ralph extended his arms. "I've been keeping up the icing." Indeed, the piping appeared rather fresh, but Leif couldn't ignore the chunks that had crumbled away. The patchwork of dough that didn't quite match. The hint of moldy fuzz along its jaw.

"It's time, Ralph. Let—" Before he could finish that thought, his phone went off. The strident jingle indicated an emergency at home. Startling seeing as how it had never gone off before.

During Leif's moment of shock, his grip loosened, and Ralph slipped away, running while cackling, "You can't catch me. I'm—"

The rat pounced on the cookie and ripped off its head. While the rodent tore into the remains, Leif checked his phone, blinked, and then whistled in disbelief at the message sent by his dad.

He escaped.

There could only be one he. And this was bad. It should have also been impossible.

Leif's magic shifted him, clothes to fur, human face and pointed ears to a reindeer with an impressive rack. While he could fly in his two-legged shape, if he wanted to move fast, he needed four.

With a galloping stride, he flung himself into the air, where it took only a moment to gather enough wind energy to give himself a burst of speed that had him back to the North Pole within a few hours. He landed on the runway just outside the perimeter of the village. Santa's Village, to be exact. His home.

As Leif cantered to a stop, he changed back to his other form, that of a male, late thirties, with dark hair long enough to cover his pointed ears for when he went out amongst the humans. Unlike others of his ilk, he didn't appreciate strangers thinking they could touch them, always asking, "Are they real?"

The eastern gate was open this time of day, guarded by elves armed with spears and, as an added precaution, a warlock as well. Old Merlo, his beard touching the ground, his pointed hat covered in stars, gave a nod as Leif passed. They didn't have many elven defensive and combat magic users. Most of their talents usually resided on the creative side of things.

Leif's long stride took him to the bright red structure that, despite no longer being used as a stable, retained its original name of Jingle Bell Barn. When the sleigh teams were phased out, it turned into a command facility for the operation of the squads that protected Santa's Village, because as the world grew so did the danger to everyone working and living in this hidden place.

Inside the barn, the stalls had been turned into offices where elves observed flickering screens: videos, social media threads, texts. They monitored as much as they could to ensure the village remained secure. Too many naughty people in the past had made attempts to invade and even take over for them to be complacent. The greedy kept coming after the incredible Plum Pudding Toy Factory that could build any toy in existence and even create some. Then there was the more recent addition of the Eggnog Electronics Facility to accommodate those asking for smartphones, video games systems, and more.

The evil someone could do if they managed to gain control of either... It couldn't be allowed, and it was up to Leif—a member of the Yule Squad—along with Mistletoe Crew and Poinsettia Posse, to ensure that never happened.

He waved to those who chirped hellos at him and made for the office of the Musher, the person who oversaw the squads. Also known as Lars Blitzen, his dad.

"What in the candy corn happened?" Leif exclaimed as he walked right on in.

Sitting at his desk, almost buried by its size, his father rubbed a hand over his weary face. "Leif, thank the Christmas Spirit you're here. We have an emergency on our hands."

"So he truly did escape?" Leif queried.

Dad nodded.

"I thought there was no way that could happen."

The statement led to his father rolling his shoulders. "By all accounts, it shouldn't have been possible. Even now we're struggling to understand. One moment, everything was fine, and then, with barely a hint of warning, the whole place came down."

"How did he escape? That pit was over a mile deep. The walls sheer ice."

"We don't think he climbed, as we didn't find any signs of it. It would appear he flew out."

"Without magic?" His understanding was Krampus had his powers taken away to ensure he could never escape his prison.

"We think he had help," his father admitted.

It took Leif a moment to recover from the shocking admission. "Who would do that?" Surely, no one in Santa's Village. The elves, reindeer, and others all knew from a young age the story of how Krampus, an evil spirit, infected Santa Claus and almost destroyed Christmas.

"I'm less worried about who and more concerned about where he has gone. We have to find him before he can do any harm."

"Shouldn't be too hard to find. Just look for reports of a large-sized monster with big freaking horns." Leif had seen the images of the monster Santa became.

Dad's lips turned down. "If he's got help, then it might not be so simple."

That arched Leif's brow. "What kind of idiot would join forces with Krampus?"

"Keep in mind, the newer generation didn't live through that time and has no idea of the horror we went through. They still believe in who he used to be, and rumor has it they want him set him free."

"Are they dumb?" Everyone knew Krampus was bad. A killer. The worst thing ever. "Haven't they studied our history? Has no one explained that Krampus isn't the original San—"

His father practically dove over the desk to slap his hand over Leif's mouth. "Shh. Don't say his name."

He pulled his father's hands from his lips and said deliberately, "Santa Claus."

"Leif!"

"You're being ridiculous. How does saying his name draw his attention?"

"I don't know, and I don't want to find out."

"Well, we don't have a choice since Krampus or Santa Claus or whatever you want to call him is on the loose. I say, if he hears and wants to come at me, let him. It would make the task of capturing him easier. You hear that, Santa? Come and get me!" he yelled to the ceiling of the room.

"Feel better?" his father asked dryly.

"Yes, because you're being crazy. He's not listening. It's only the song that claims he can hear us all the time. You yourself told me that's not true."

"That aspect of the legend wasn't true of him before. I'm not sure about the thing he's become."

"Let's assume for a moment he didn't suddenly acquire extra powers. That would mean he can't hear us unless he's in the room or using a spell. More importantly, he has no idea about naughty or good either."

"And? I don't see why that's important."

"Because, if Krampus keeps to his usual style and goes after the naughty, then he is going to need The List." The List being the Holy Grail for Christmas. Updated daily all year round and heavily guarded, only accessible to a few people.

"Already thought of that. Candy Cane Central went on high alert the moment we got word of his escape. As an added precaution, Mistletoe Crew is guarding Allie Snowball." The current curator of the naughty-and-nice book.

"Now, don't freak out, because I have to ask. I don't suppose there a chance he's returned to his jolly self?" Leif had never met the original Santa Claus, only heard the stories passed down by his dad, who'd served under the big man before his demise.

No one quite knew what happened. How had Santa left himself open enough to be infected? Some believed the weakening of his powers began with the baby boomers. The explosion of families. So many gifts, the North Pole couldn't keep up. It led to the creation of their first factory, as the elves pivoted to keep up with demand for the good children who'd earned a present.

Along with the increased good came the bad. Record numbers of naughty kids entered The List. Some theorized it broke Santa's spirit and led to him turning into the monster that became known as Krampus. Not that anyone knew at first that Santa was infected.

Previously, when Krampus infected someone, he had only his host's abilities to draw upon. Humans gave him flesh and a limit to his strength. But when Krampus slipped inside Santa—who chose to sacrifice himself rather than see someone else become host and start the cycle again—he found power. It was said the monster learned how to mimic the big man. His laugh. His smile. He even fooled Mrs. Claus for a while.

It took years, and the death of many, before the elves finally pieced it together, that the person killing the bad children on their list was the jolly man himself. The elves and all those who worked in the village banded together to end Krampus's reign of terror.

Since they feared killing Santa's body would unleash Krampus to find another body, they instead chose to strip the magic from Santa and put him in a prison he couldn't escape. Forever locked away that no more children would die.

Bereft at the loss of her husband, Mrs. Claus left not long after, never to be seen again.

And the elves...

Went on without Santa.

The sled and reindeer were retired in favor of a drone system in conjunction with a portal that allowed them to literally deposit presents under the tree. No need to fly around the world at ludicrous speed. No more risking life or limb. Some people forgot to confine their pets for the night, and more than a few elves returned with bite marks and haunted expressions. The stories they told about some cats had even the adult elves hugging each other.

Life went on without Santa and, until now, had run rather smoothly.

"I'm afraid Krampus is still as dangerous as before," his father said, replying to his last query. "Possibly even worse given the decades he spent alone."

"If you have The List covered, then what do you want me to do?" Because his father would never waste Leif's talents on mundane guard duty, not when he was one of the few who could move among humans without undue notice. A taller than normal elf at almost five foot ten, Leif towered over most, even his father, a pure-blood elf who was an almost unheard of four foot eleven. Leif's height mostly came from his mother's side. His reindeer uncles, Sven and Mikhail, were both almost six feet.

His father appeared grim as he announced, "You need to find Krampus before he ruins Christmas."

CHAPTER
TWO

IN A LITTLE TOWN, IN A CUTE SHOP, FLUFFING A SHIRT EMBLAZONED WITH A MUG WITH A SMILEY FACE: 'I RUN ON COFFEE AND CHRISTMAS CHEER.'

I might just wear that shirt tomorrow. Bella finished smoothing the bright red fabric of the sweater she'd just placed on the mannequin. It would draw the attention of people as they passed by the window. Once they came inside, they often left with more than just a shirt.

Adding a clothing line with quirky holiday messages brought in a very nice revenue stream. Not to mention there was something kind of joyful about seeing return clients wearing their version of holiday cheer. The world could use more smiles and goodwill.

For herself, Bella wore a lovely pastel-hued knitted sweater with interlinking snowflakes. Some called it hideous and laughed while asking where they could buy one. They wanted it because they thought it ugly, even as it was Bella's favorite. Her mom made it.

From a young age, Mom had bestowed in Bella a love of Christmas. Shown her how to be giving. Kept her spirit bright even when things tried to turn her smile upside down.

In the days leading up to Christmas, they'd bake and decorate, sing and watch corny movies that made her sigh happily. Mom turned Christmas into the best time of the year. A mother who would be arriving in a few days to spend the holidays.

It had been so long since she'd seen her. Three whole months! Although it helped they talked in person every day.

When Mom started travelling the world after Bella left for college, she had worried they wouldn't remain close. She should have known better. Mom remained in touch not only by phone but by helping Bella's business thrive by locating and shipping back unique Christmas treasures. The latest box sat in the back; however, she'd sworn to herself she wouldn't open it until she finished the new display in her front window, which took longer than it should have given her distraction. Blame the sports car she'd seen pulling to the curb across the street. It had bright red wheel rims, the body of it a deep emerald that caught her eye given the green reminded her of a fresh pine tree waiting for decoration.

Speaking of waiting, that front window wouldn't frost itself. She held up her can and shook, giving it her everything because she didn't have a spare and her window would look terrible if she ran out partway.

A man stepped out of the car and stood by it, glancing around, eyeing the shops nearby. They were mostly converted brownstones, the main floor holding a store or restaurant and the upstairs reserved for living quarters. He wore a long, dark coat, the kind worn by those guys in *The Matrix*. Very cool looking. Add in sunglasses and dark emerald boots and he was super interesting, hence why Bella paused the shaking of her can to stare. He didn't look like the type to be interested in choosing his own freshly baked goods, yet he headed for the bakery across from her, which had recently combined the amazing cupcake side of the business with to-die-for bread on the other.

Since she'd moved in a few months ago, she'd developed a love and hate relationship with the goodies, also known as her hips' nemesis. Each mouthwatering indulgence meant at least an hour exercising with her Oculus, fighting off villains with her light saber as she role-played in an Empire far, far away. To those that might mock her chosen form of fitness? Her mantra clearly stated exercise should be fun, and slaying those aligned with the Dark Side sure as heck put a smile on her face.

Just before the door to Oral Orgasm—the name they should have given the place of delicious treats instead of The Hexed Goodies—the man paused and glanced over his shoulder.

Right at Bella.

Being the friendly sort, she waved and smiled. He cocked his head as she pressed the button on her can.

Pffft. It spat a few drops.

Oh dear. Please don't let it be a dud.

She shook it hard and pressed again. This time not a thing emerged.

She wiped the nozzle against the denim fabric of her pants and pushed down hard on the nozzle button. At first nothing, then the cap shot off and artificial snow exploded in a spatter.

Luckily her glasses prevented it from getting in her eyes, but it didn't taste good when she accidentally licked her lips. A good thing the stuff was washable. She rubbed her sleeve over her glasses to clear the lenses and failed miserably, as it smeared, so she removed the glasses and lifted her sweater to find her clean T-shirt, a better fabric for wiping.

Once she cleared the lenses, she jammed them back on her face, pivoted to exit the window, slipped and landed on the manger, and splayed across baby Jesus—who happened to be an adorable Grogu.

"Sorry, Baby Yoda," she muttered. She took a deep breath and hoped nobody saw as she pushed herself upward. A glance through the window showed the man in the duster staring slack-jawed.

She might have been embarrassed but for the fact she'd always been clumsy. Her mother said she'd been born with two left feet, and those feet conspired against her at every chance. She almost did the splits on the way out of the window display because she managed to step in more of the slick snow and tumbled into her store. In good news, she didn't break anything. Her teachers would be impressed. In school, her teachers quickly learned to keep Bella far from the edges of the stage for school concerts. Otherwise, she always managed to fall off.

Mom would laugh when it happened and say she was just like her dad, a dad Bella never knew because he died before she was born.

She headed for the back room to clean up and passed the box her mom had shipped. It was a wooden crate instead of the usual taped cardboard. It had fragile written on it and hummed with magic. Mom had splurged for a spelled seal against tampering, a neat new innovation that reduced incidents of missing packages. Apparently, tagging thieves with flashing words on their forehead that said "Arrest Me" had that effect.

Using magic to mark those up to no good had been gaining traction within government circles since the zombie animal incident caused by a necromancer the previous year. Many said had the necromancer been identified the moment she raised the dead she could have been stopped before she tried to zombify the world.

Bella had moved to town well after all the undead excitement, taking advantage of the surge of vacant properties at low prices. Mom hadn't been impressed given she'd been trying to convince Bella to move down south to Mexico. Nice place. Warm and tropical, but not somewhere she wanted to live, mostly because they rarely got snow in the lower altitudes. Bella couldn't imagine a Christmas without it! Give her fluffy flakes, iced-over ponds, and people bundled against the cold as they strolled. At times she debated moving farther north where the winter season lasted longer.

In the back room, she washed off the exploded gook from her skin, stripped off her top, and put on a new

Christmas shirt, this one with a fireplace and the phrase: Hot for Christmas.

The shop bell rang as she dabbed at the white blobs in her hair. She spent the next few hours handling customers. December was a busy time for her for obvious reasons. Around seven, things died down and she closed up shop, noticing as she flipped her sign that the car remained out front. The lights in the tasty food shop had dimmed, while those on the floor above were bright. The man in the fancy car must know the owners, Mindy and her fiancé, Reiver. Bella had met them once. Handsome couple. Rumor had it he was a former Cryptid Authority agent, which she had her doubts about. Who went from fighting cryptid crime to baking bread?

Then again, who cared, given the amount of traffic it brought the street. It had been one of the reasons she'd chosen this location after her last rental two states over proved problematic. Mainly it burned to the ground and the landlord blamed the tree she kept decorated and lit year-round. While he might have been correct about the origin of the fire, the cause wasn't her fault. According to the investigation, someone tossed a malfunctioning vape at it, but she got the blame. The building mostly suffered smoke damage, but everyone got evicted.

Rather than deal with a new landlord, Bella, with Mom's help, went looking for a place she could own. Since she didn't have the best budget, a town recovering from a necromancer attack provided a cost-effective solution that had already paid off due to foot traffic drawn to the bakery across the street. She'd already tripled her profits for the year, meaning her bad luck turned out to be great!

The switch just inside the door to the storage room at the back turned off the overhead lights, and she took a moment to smile at the bright bulbs framing her front window and the smaller ones glinting in her potted tree. She didn't believe in cutting them down and killing them. Although she did wonder what she'd do once it grew too tall. Perhaps Mindy, who didn't just bake treats but was also an Earth Witch, could help her.

Must be cool to have magic. All Bella had was an abundance of Christmas spirit.

She checked the door on the alley, even as she knew she'd not opened it that day. She didn't have an alarm system yet. Hadn't seen the need. She relied on an old-fashioned bell on her door. An antique door that still had the brass mail slot, which also had a string running to a bell when the flap opened.

Before heading up the stairs to the second floor where she had an apartment, another bonus to this building she'd bought, she snared the package from Mom. All day long she'd been dying to open it. After the day she'd had, she'd earned the box.

As she opened her apartment door, she beamed at her pet. "Hey, Big Fluff." She'd tried various names on her long-haired feline, adopted a few years ago when she'd found her shivering in an alley on Christmas Eve. When no one came forth to claim her, she'd decided to keep the cat who rejected every single appellation until, in frustration, Bella exploded with, "You need a name, Big Fluff."

The reply? A meow and a suddenly purring kitty rubbing against her lower legs.

"Are you hungry, my precious?" For those wondering, she softened her tone when speaking to her majesty. Big Fluff expected a certain level of respect and worship.

The cat stretched and yawned before sauntering to the small kitchen area. Bella placed the package on the breakfast counter before opening the fridge for the fish she'd grabbed from the market on her lunch break. When she'd returned to run it up to her fridge, her cat hadn't even deigned to open an eye where she basked in the sunlight on the window ledge. Now, however, kitty almost trotted as the smell of salmon permeated the air.

The cat got almost fresh fish while Bella went for a nice hot soup, crackers, and bread pudding for dessert. Not a big dinner, but if she got hungry, she had some chestnuts she could roast on the fire. Imagine her delight when she'd discovered the old building had retained the original fireplace on the second floor.

Belly full, and the cat stretched out for her evening nap, she finally could tackle the mysterious crate.

Scissors wouldn't do the trick. Her tongue poked between teeth and lips as she pried at the wooden lid with a crowbar kept by her bed just in case the zombies came back.

The wooden lid popped off just as her phone rang. She eyed the straw then the screen, which showed a smiling Mom calling.

She hit answer and speakerphone. "Hey, Mom, what's shaking?"

"My booty because the salsa music downstairs is slamming."

Bella smiled as her mom did her best to sound hip and cool. "Maybe you can find yourself a hot dance partner. I'd be okay if you gave me a daddy for Christmas." A thing she'd often teased, and yet her mother had never dated, stating she'd only ever love one man.

"Maybe you'll get your wish," trilled her mom.

The surprise reply dropped her jaw. "Wait, what? Did you meet someone?"

"Not exactly and not why I'm calling. Did you get a box from me?"

"Yes. I was just about to open it."

"Don't."

"What?"

"You need to wait for me. What's inside that box requires special handling."

"You do recall I deal in fragile things on a daily basis, right?" Bella couldn't help the sarcasm.

"Fine, if you must know, it's your Christmas present."

"Really?" She eyed the straw with even more interest.

"Yes really, so no snooping. I need to be there when you open it."

It killed Bella to mumble, "I won't peek, promise."

"That's my good girl. Now, tell me about your day."

As Bella launched into a recitation of her clumsiness, she sat in her favorite chair, afghan over her legs, cat in her lap, a gentle snow falling outside. By the time she hung up with Mom, she'd almost forgotten the box.

Okay, no she hadn't. Giddy excitement filled her as she wondered what it held. Mom always managed to find the best gifts. She couldn't wait for Christmas morning.

It was going to be epic!

CHAPTER
THREE

WEARING HIS SPECIAL PACKAGE BOXERS A
WEEK BEFORE CHRISTMAS...

AND LEIF HAD YET TO CATCH A BREAK.

After his father gave him the mission of seeking out Santa, he'd gone to the barn and asked that, along with reports of any Krampus sightings, he wanted any Santa Claus ones, too. He'd gotten predictable laughter.

Joy, their top information gatherer, had shaken her head, sending braids woven with ribbon flying. "Do you know how many hits we get in an hour of the big man in red? We're going to need specifics. Where he might have gone. Who he might see."

Problem being no one knew where Santa had fled to. As to who he might try and find... Everyone he once knew lived in Santa's Village. Okay, maybe not everyone. Mrs. Claus, for instance, had left and never been seen again. And there were the occasional elves who also departed looking for a change. But Santa wouldn't know how to find them. Heck, he wouldn't know most of the people in the village anymore given how many decades had passed. Santa might live forever, but elves, while having a longer life span than humans, didn't.

"Any suggestions on how we can find Krampus?"

"The news," Joy suggested. "They'll report if he starts killing."

A good plan. After all, the last time Krampus hunted, the murders had been obvious.

The plan failed quickly, given they'd not realized just how bad the world had gotten. The things they saw disheartened the usually happy elves.

And it was for nothing. They didn't find Krampus.

With time running out, Leif needed a clue. So he went to the library and hit the books that centered around the history of Santa's descent into Krampus.

The accounts of that time proved sparse, as if the historian couldn't bear to give words to what happened. Santa got infected and went bad. The elves imprisoned him. No mention of how. No details on where they captured him.

Given Leif's father had lived through that time, he tried questioning him, only to come away further puzzled because no matter how he asked, his father didn't stray from his story.

"We trapped Krampus in the pit under the glacier."

The same story was repeated by everyone he approached who'd been alive during that time. Which made no sense. Surely someone recalled how the whole Krampus capture had gone down.

There were many paintings of a big man dressed in red, battling a monstrous creature with horns and hooved feet. A battle Santa always won until he became the infected. Or should Leif call it possessed? After all, Krampus could jump from body to body, and apparently even the strongest couldn't fight him. How else to explain how a man who loved children could suddenly turn into a monster in the days before Christmas, killing and causing so much grief and evil?

Which made him wonder, why did Santa only appear to turn savage just before the big day? Was it important?

When he asked his dad how Santa appeared after Christmas and the killing, his father had shrugged. *"Seemed like himself. Maybe a little more agitated once we hit the countdown from twelve. But we assumed he was worrying about the job."*

What was it about Christmas that agitated Krampus into violence?

And why did no one remember much of that time? The elves close to Santa in those final years appeared to have had much of their memories suppressed or erased, indicating a secret that they feared getting out. Surely someone recalled. Perhaps the person who'd wiped their knowledge?

Given the sparse details in the village, Leif hit the internet and dug through the human stories featuring Krampus, a monster who first made an appearance centuries ago, killing naughty children at Christmas. In those stories Krampus was just a monster. Nothing about infection causing a person to kill until the more modern versions of the tale, many of which the monster won.

With the internet just making Krampus into an even murkier figure, he tried talking to those who'd taken a stint guarding Krampus's prison. They had little to relate. A few admitted they'd been discomfited. A few claimed nightmares and phantom voices. The only survivor of Krampus's escape recalled nothing once her shift started.

The prison had been reduced to a hole in the ice. Satellite imaging showed the gash into the ground that went a mile deep supposedly. Leif couldn't know for sure since the prison lacked any record of being built. There was also no time limit placed on the incarceration. No indication anyone ever checked on him. Nothing about how his magic was removed or where it went. Probably to ensure Krampus didn't get his monstrous hands on it.

It appeared someone had helped him escape. Who would do such a thing? It boggled the mind. Could it be that group his father mentioned? Someone who thought Krampus should be set free. How could he find someone to talk to about it?

When research didn't get him any answers, Leif finally resorted to the one thing he'd been avoiding. He visited the Abominable Seer, Daphne.

The seer lived in a cave of ice a fair distance from Santa's village because she claimed their lights were too bright. She had a point.

A snow yeti, Daphne loomed almost ten feet, her stocky frame covered in fur, a female with a silvery blue hue to her hair who could speak the language of humans. Every single one it was said.

Being a seer, she could give a person hints of the future. Clues to what they sought. Best of all, she asked no price for any of her knowledge.

So why his reluctance on seeing her?

The smell hit him a mile out.

Daphne had been feeding on the seal population again. It always gave her the farts. Eye-watering, stomach-churning. The particularly bad ones could start smoldering clothes and singeing hairs.

A bandana covered Leif's lower face. and he wore goggles as he passed the frozen wasteland outside her cave. Pitted ice and desiccated bones. Nothing lived in a mile radius of her home.

He reached the massive cave with its miasma of yellow green wafting forth, pungent enough to penetrate even the magic barrier fused to his mask.

He warned her of his approach. "Hello, Daphne. It is I—"

"It's Leif, I know." She emerged, a massive creature wearing a sarong style sheet of fabric and lipstick on her fangs that looked a lot like dripping blood. "I've known you'd be visiting for weeks now."

"Then you know why I'm here."

"*He* has escaped." She shook her arms, and bangles jangled.

"Yes, he has. Can you see where he is?"

She shook her head. "Hidden from me. Hidden from you. Hidden from everyone who seeks him."

"Meaning you can't help." His lips turned down.

"Help?" She tittered. "I see things. I see you going on

a trip. Vroom!" Daphne strode past him, arms waving, almost skipping, the impact hard enough to cause crunching and cracking of the hardened ice and snow below her feet.

"A trip to where?" Guiding Daphne to the little details could save time later.

"A place where the dead were alive and two of the extinct were born again, and you will find what you need."

"The name of that place is…" he prompted.

"Destiny!" Daphne pirouetted and laughed, even as her actions caused a mini avalanche of ice to fall from a nearby glacier.

Since she kept avoiding answering his query, he changed tactic. "Will I find *him* there?"

"Everything you need. Everything you've ever wanted." Daphne stopped moving and stared at him. "You will save Christmas."

"I'd love to do that, but it would help if I knew where I had to go."

"Yummy cupcake store." Daphne smacked her lips.

"That doesn't exactly narrow it down by much given how many exist in the world."

"How is your friend Reiver?"

"Wait, what?" The sudden change of subject had him blinking. What did Reiver—an old friend he'd made from his time at the Cryptid Authority Training Academy—have to do with anything? "Will Reiver be able to help me?"

Rather than reply, her lips quirked as she said, "Love will save the day."

"What's love got to do with it?" he yelled as she went bounding away on the ice.

"Everything," was her booming reply, along with an explosive fart that sent him sprinting for safety.

As he trudged back to Santa's Village, he went over what Daphne said. Much of it didn't make sense yet, but one part stood out.

Reiver.

A man who had recently retired because he'd met someone. Even more astonishing, Reiver went from hunter for the CA—the Cryptid Authority in charge of policing all things that freaked out humans—to baker in a small town that had, according to recent news, defeated a necromancer and supposedly uncovered a dragon's lair.

Could this be where he'd save Christmas?

Only one way to find out.

He flew on four legs until he entered airspace that didn't take kindly to unauthorized flyers. He then took two commercial flights the rest of the way. Upon his arrival, knowing he couldn't fly by day without being noticed, he chose to splurge by renting the fastest and sleekest car he could find.

The bakery proved easy to find. It was located right across the street from a store titled Holiday Cheer with its façade painted white, the sign bright red and green, matching the door and the window frame. As he took it all in, he caught a woman in the window, doing her best to maim herself decorating it, her clumsiness like nothing he'd ever seen.

When she managed to escape, more or less unscathed, he entered his friend's shop and began immediately drooling at the smell of the bread and so much more.

A young teen behind the counter lifted their head and smiled. "Can I help you?"

"Hi. Maybe you can. I'm looking for Reiver."

Before the kid could reply, a voice rasped, "Well, I'll be damned. Look who's come visiting. I'm surprised given how close it is to Christmas."

Leif smiled at the other man. "I wish this was a social call. Is there somewhere we can talk?"

"Follow me. We can talk in the kitchen. Mindy's already back there."

Indicating Reiver wanted her to hear whatever Leif had to say. Leif knew better than to question. He'd long trusted this man, and besides, while he'd only briefly met Reiver's wife at the wedding, it might be a good idea to bring her in given she was an Earth Witch. The Earth Mother tended to be particular about who she blessed.

The moment Mindy saw Leif leaning against a clean metal counter, chewing on the powdered sugar pretzel Reiver insisted he try, she smiled wide. "Leif, so nice to see you again. I've heard so much about you. An actual reindeer from Santa's Village. How utterly amazing."

He shot a glance at Reiver, who rolled his shoulders and muttered, "Don't look at me. I didn't spill the beans. I told her you worked for a secret CA agency."

"Don't blame him." Mindy jumped in to defend Reiver. "I was just infusing some cookies with a stay-awake hex, my foot in the dirt, when Mother Earth told me your secret."

"What exactly did she say?" he asked, not entirely surprised to hear about Earth Mother's interest. Many elves worshipped her, even more since Santa went to prison. Leif wasn't a strict follower, but his parents were. Mom claimed that with the loss of Santa and Mrs. Claus, the elves needed someone to believe in. Mother Earth, with her devotion to all things living, seemed the perfect fit.

"She said you're here on an important mission and to help you as much as we can."

"Oh. Good."

"So what's the problem? What can we do to aid?" Reiver asked.

Leif could have launched into a complicated explanation, but he didn't believe in beating around the holly bush. "I'm here because your town might be the key to saving Christmas."

A deep silence fell the moment Leif told his friend he'd come to save Christmas.

As Reiver digested the words, Mindy clapped her hands. "Sounds like we're going to need more than cupcakes and pretzels for this."

The pair spoke to their staff handling the sales before leading the way upstairs, the railing wound with a vine that shivered as they passed. They emerged into living quarters that smelled like spring, the many plants all around thriving in the sunshine spilling through the many windows. It appeared they'd knocked through walls to create an open space for all the greenery. Some of which he'd swear whispered. Relaxation hit Leif. He'd not realized just what a ribbon wrapped bundle of nerves he was until his muscles eased.

"Coffee? Tea?"

"I don't suppose you have hot cocoa?" Leif asked. He avoided caffeine but needed sugar.

"A hot cocoa sounds delicious." Mindy grabbed her pregnant belly and smiled wide. "Marshmallows?"

"Oh yes."

"How do you feel about a cinnamon sprinkle on top?"

His turn to smile wide. "It's a good thing you're taken," he teased.

Reiver slid an arm around Mindy. "Yes, she is, so find your own."

The very idea had him snorting. "Not all of us are built for domestic bliss."

"What I thought, too, until I met the right person."

"Ha." Mindy snorted. "The first time we met you were killing zombies."

"After I caught you when you fell from the second floor of your house."

Her cheeks turned pink. "You might have been a little heroic."

Reiver arched a brow.

She chuckled in reply before winking at Leif. "Let's leave it at our meeting was definitely unconventional and unexpected. So never say never. Now, give me a second, and I shall give you a hot cocoa to knock your socks off."

"I'll get the cocoas. Sit." Reiver put a hand in the middle of her back to offer a gentle guide, but she remained stubbornly planted.

"I am not an invalid."

"I know your feet are sore."

"My feet are always sore. I stand. A lot."

"Fine. Do it. And don't forget some of your cookies," Reiver grumbled before dropping onto the couch.

As Leif settled across on the club chair, he remarked, "It's like you want her to kill you."

An unrepentant Reiver grinned. "I knew she wouldn't let me do it. But..."

"You had to make the attempt." Leif chuckled and shook his head. "You both seem very happy."

"We are. But you're not here to admire my perfect life. What's this about saving Christmas? Actually, don't tell me yet. Let me give Mindy a hand bringing over the snack."

A few groans of pleasure later, as Leif inhaled quite possibly one of the best hot cocoas ever and snacked on a plate of salty crackers and cheese, accompanied with sweet confections, he told them just about everything. Who Krampus was. What he'd done. How he'd been imprisoned. The escape.

They listened with wide eyes as he took the story right up to Daphne's cryptic message—minus the farts.

Finished with, "...and if we don't find him, something terrible will happen to Christmas."

Mindy stared at him and muttered, "I can't believe Santa Claus is real."

"Is. Was. The man who used to bring such joy became the worst kind of monster."

"A monster that should have been handled by the CA," Reiver interjected. "The fact Krampus keeps returning indicates it's a parasite. Until we eradicate the root, the problem will never end."

"Hence why the Village imprisoned rather than kill him."

"Krampus should have been analyzed."

"Too dangerous."

"According to who?" Reiver queried.

"Everyone."

"And yet, no one seems to remember much of Krampus at all, so how do you know that's true?"

Leif frowned. "Elves can't lie."

"Okay, then let me ask you, you don't find it odd no one ever seemingly spoke to or even checked on him?"

The reminder had Leif shifting in his seat. "I did find that strange, but at the same time, if it's some kind of infection, they probably worried it would jump from Santa to someone else."

"Sounds more like a demon than a virus to me," Reiver stated.

"Either or, it was probably wise to keep their distance, as they couldn't be sure that anyone visiting Krampus wouldn't leave infected." Mindy took the side of the Village.

Reiver shook his head. "All the more reason it should

have been studied. Now it's escaped and we have no idea how to handle it."

"The CA doesn't have any info on Krampus?"

"None, so we'll be starting from scratch."

We'll? He caught that word. "You'll help then?"

"Fuck yeah. This is Christmas we're talking about. If it's okay, I'm going to call my friend in the history department and have him dig up anything they can find. None of this fictional stuff on the internet and television."

Mindy appeared serious as she said, "Should we speak to priests and priestesses? If this is some kind of demon or evil spirit, maybe it needs to be ordered to leave."

Leif's expression brightened. "You mean perform an exorcism." A crazy idea that lit all his happy holiday bulbs because, what if they didn't find Krampus but managed to free Santa?

"Exorcism, or extraction." Mindy shrugged. "There has to be way of removing it and ensuring it never harms again."

Leif rubbed his hands. "I see why I was sent here. Where should we start?"

And that was the question to stump them all. They pondered it over a breaded and flavorful chicken served on a bed of handmade egg noodles in a carbonara coating with bacon chunks and, on the side, charred asparagus spears. It wasn't a turkey dinner with all the fixings, but Leif still hummed.

They didn't go to bed late, the baking duo having an

early start time. Leif got the spare room with a window overlooking the street. He stood at it for a while, watching the lights across the way that reminded him of home. Upstairs, the largest window remained bright. He wondered if the clumsy woman he'd seen earlier lived over the shop like Mindy and Reiver did with theirs.

Not that it mattered. Leif was here to do a job and once done, he'd return to the North Pole. Alone.

He sighed. It would be nice to have someone to cuddle by the fire and roast chestnuts while watching a Christmas classic. As he saw a shooting star blink across the sky, he even made a wish.

CHAPTER
FOUR

WEARING A COMFORTABLE SWEATER WITH THE WORDS "OH HOLY NIGHT" AND A WINKING STAR...

The movie ended with Christmas being saved, and Bella sighed happily. She'd loved those kinds of stories her entire life. Goodwill and love prevailing always filled her with warmth. Speaking of hot, she glanced down at Big Fluff currently shedding on her lap, slightly digging in her claws, warning Bella of the danger if she moved without permission.

"I have to pee," she stated.

Big Fluff snuggled in deeper and put pressure on her bladder.

Wise to her tricks, Bella knew what to do next. "Does someone need a late-night snack?"

The large kitty took a second to ponder before slinking off her lap and heading for the kitchen, tail held high. Bella knew better than to make her highness wait. She went straight for the cat milk and poured some in a dish then heated it for twenty-three seconds. Only once

Big Fluff had her face in the bowl did she bolt for the bathroom.

Upon emerging, she paused by the window overlooking the street below. A gentle snow fell, so pretty this time of night. Her lights and those across the way provided colorful illumination, enough to see movement across the road, furtive and strange, a person hunched within a cloak. They paused by the car parked in front of the bakery and spent a moment studying it before the hooded head turned in her direction. Bella pulled away from the window, not wanting to spy. Unease filled her. The hair on her nape lifted as if lightning coiled, readying to strike.

It wasn't a bolt of electricity that hit but a cat.

Big Fluff suddenly yowled and swiped at her leg, causing Bella to squeak as she dodged out of the way.

"I'm sorry. I didn't realize you wanted your window bed."

The cat offered an unimpressed sniff before climbing onto the cushion that overlooked the street.

Bella glanced out once more to see the cloaked figure gone but the window for the bakery smashed, upright shards clearly visible.

Oh no. That person had been up to no good.

Before she could react, she heard the chime of a bell. By its strident note it was the one attached to the mail slot on her shop door, wide enough to accommodate items up to three inches thick. But she wasn't expecting a delivery, and she'd never known anyone to drop off things this late.

Could it be a rodent? She hoped not. The last time Big Fluff had decided to be a cat and catch an invading pest, she'd destroyed a few unique fragile items in the process. Bella didn't have the heart to scold the pleased feline when she dropped the heaving mouse at her feet before shaking the glass from her fur.

She eyed the napping cat. Perhaps she should check it out on her own first.

Just in case, Bella armed herself with a broom, not that she'd have the nerve to whack with it, but she did have a weird belief she could sweep a critter back out into the street.

The door at the bottom of the stairs remained closed and unlocked. She'd never seen the need to bolt it once she closed the shop for the day. She eased it open and listened, strained her ears for nothing. Perhaps the mail slot had suffered a strong gust of wind. Despite trying to come up with reasons to go back to her apartment, she crept into the shop, aiming for the glow of her tree.

Tink-tink-tink. A few notes from the musical carousel the register played. Odd since it usually required cranking to make any sound at all. A glance at the intricate antique didn't show anybody playing with it. Logic dictated she remained alone. The shop door was locked. The larger bell for it silent. As for the alley door, she never took the bar off it unless she was putting garbage in the dumpster, always in daylight. People might claim the goblins scavenging them were harmless, but that was only because they didn't know the truth. Goblins were what happened to elves who went bad. She'd accidentally seen the movie and been scarred by it since.

Scuff.

The distinct noise had her butt cheeks clenching tight. Bella didn't do scary. She closed her eyes if a movie or show even hinted at having a terrifying part.

She took a deep breath. Reminded herself it was most likely a rodent, maybe even an adorable squirrel looking for a warm place to hide. At the thought, she eyed the tree, wondering if a woodland creature had made itself at home, and if yes, would it be open to wearing clothing? Because a squirrel in a Santa suit would be adorable.

She tiptoed far enough into her shop to see all four corners, pivoting slowly, broom clutched in sweaty fingers. Body taut with tension.

Why was she so afraid?

She did her best to relax, thrusting her shoulders back, taking a deep breath. "It's okay little whatever you are. Come on out. I won't hurt you. If you're hungry, I have a bag of toffee-covered peanuts behind the counter."

The inanity of talking to a possible squirrel. As if it would understand or reply. Perhaps if she shook out some nuts, it would discern her intent.

Snick.

The faint dragging sound drew her attention. Nothing at eye level. Her gaze dropped to the tree and the skirt under it with the empty boxes wrapped as presents. She almost missed seeing the gingerbread cookie figurine, its brown body decorated in red and green icing, its eyes black dots, its mouth a flat red line, the buttons marching down its belly a green that matched the piping giving it slippers on its feet. It brandished a fork.

She blinked.

The gingerbread man with the tined utensil remained, but the weird thing? It wasn't one of her decorations. She'd never buy something so terrifying. Had someone planted it in her store?

Who cared why? It didn't belong. She bent down to grab the figurine, only to gasp as it thrust the fork in her direction and squeaked, "Touch me and die!"

She straightened with a rounded mouth. Surely, she was dreaming. Cookies did not talk. Or threaten. Was it battery operated?

"Where is it?" it asked in a high-pitched voice.

"Where is what?" she replied even as she struggled to grasp she spoke with baked goods.

"Give it!" The cookie aimed the fork in Bella's direction.

"No idea what you want, and I have to say, I don't like your tone." Gingerbread cookies were supposed to be yummy holiday treats, not threatening baked goods.

"Give!" It jabbed, and before it could stab her in the ankle, she reached and snared the fork, dangling the figure holding it off the ground.

"Bad cookie," she chided.

Judging by its slashed brows, it felt no chagrin. It hung from the fork and hooted, a weird noise that only chilled her when it got a reply.

More than a few actually.

A glance down showed her suddenly surrounded by more gingerbread cookies, all brandishing utensils and a few with metal skewers.

Uh-oh.

The ring of cookies closed in, and Bella readied to step over them—after all, they were less than eight inches tall—when there was a clatter of things falling.

Blame Big Fluff, who knocked things down as she performed a less than graceful leap at the impossibly alive cookies.

"Cat!" yodeled the instigator hanging from the fork in her grip. Before it could act, Big Fluff swiped, and while there was no blood, as the cookie body and head separated, it went inert.

Screams of rage erupted as the remaining cookies attacked her cat!

"Don't panic, baby! I'll save you." Bella still held the broom and swept at the menace.

When they kept swarming back, she resorted to the fork in her other hand, leaning down and stabbing at the cookies threatening her kitty and her ankles.

She apologized each time she speared one.

"Sorry."

"Pardon."

"Please don't gnaw your arm off."

Kitty accounted for more than a few demolished baked goods—because it soon became clear she dealt with actual cookies. Once the fighting stopped, they were left circled in crumbs and chunks of gingerbread.

"Oh dear. What a mess." A part of her realized she was in shock, but that didn't stop her from muttering, "I'll need a dustpan to go with this broom." She left her cat batting at inert pieces to run upstairs and grab cleaning supplies. She skipped back down, almost falling the last few steps as Big Fluff went bolting through her legs.

"Slow down. I wasn't stealing your spot in the window," she grumbled as she headed back into the shop to clean. Now that she was thinking more calmly, it occurred she should probably also call the Cryptid Authority. They might want to hear about rampaging gingerbread cookies. Or would they think her crazy? It wasn't as if she had proof unless the broken chunks counted.

As she entered the shop, she paused. Where had the mess gone? The floor was bare. Not a single crumb to be seen.

Had she imagined the attack?

Possible. She'd heard of hex pranks, the kind that caused hallucinations, but why target her? And how come it felt so real?

Real enough she headed for the front door to check the lock and secure the mail slot, the metal clip giving her a hard time as she wrenched it into place. Nothing would be getting in now.

The glow of the tree at her back dimmed, and she whirled to see why.

"Eep." The only thing she could say. She'd found the answer to the missing crumbs as she faced a monster of zombie cookie chunks and icing.

The giant gingerbread man reached for Bella, and she shrieked. Which did nothing to help. The cookie opened its mouth wide, and she didn't want to find out if it could actually chomp her.

She whirled and fiddled with the locks she'd just checked, grunting as a gingerbread arm swept into her and knocked her aside. She scrambled to her knees and crawled into the storefront window, looking for the candy cane garden stakes she'd put in there earlier. She grabbed one and whirled just as the gingerbread flopped atop her.

She impaled it on the swirled metal decoration. It went right through the giant cookie, and while it didn't scream, its jagged brows slanted angrily. It rounded its mouth and hissed, "Where. Is. It?"

Still had no idea what it meant, and rather than find out, Bella bunched her knees under the cookie and heaved, shoving it away from her, the garden stake jutting from its body. It recovered too quickly and uttered a high-pitched screech of rage.

Her least favorite treat for Christmas charged. At the last minute, she stepped aside, but the cookie snared her in passing as it broke the window.

CHAPTER
FIVE

WONDERING IF HE SHOULD HAVE WORN HIS OFFICIAL ELF GEAR REPLETE WITH POINTY SLIPPERS...

Leif lay in the guest bed, wondering what he'd do on the morrow. He'd found Reiver like the seer suggested. Now what? It wasn't long until Christmas and—

Crash. The distinct sound of breaking glass immediately caught Leif's attention. He lay in the bed only for a moment before rolling from it and dressing as well as arming himself.

He opened his bedroom door to find Reiver already in the hall. "Don't you dare come downstairs."

Mindy protested. "I can help."

"Or you can let me handle it."

"Not alone." Mindy stood in their bedroom door, arms crossed, looking stubborn.

"Don't worry. I've got Leif. You need to protect the bun in your oven."

"I'm not fragile," she grumbled, her hair lifting as if caught in an invisible storm.

"No, you're not, but our child is. I'll call for help if it's more than I can handle."

"You'd better," she warned.

Reiver gave her a swift kiss before heading down the stairs, Leif at his heels. At the bottom, Leif muttered, "You, ask for help?"

Reiver snorted. "Never, and she knows that, which means we've got only until she pees before she's down here, so let's get shit under control before then. The alarm was triggered because of a broken roadside window."

"Alarm? Do you often get break-ins?"

"Not since we put in security. We had problems for a while with those thinking they could steal and resell Mindy's hexed cupcakes on the black market."

"So much naughty in the world," Leif murmured softly. The door into the kitchen didn't make a sound, and they quickly made their way into the sweets shop, where a gust of wind brought in flakes from the outside.

"There's no one here," Leif stated unnecessarily. Reiver would have known the moment he did.

His friend still took a cautious look around behind the counter, even glancing overhead, whereas Leif toed the empty boxes spilled on the floor. "Looks like they were after the cookies." While he and Reiver had caught up, Mindy had been finishing up the decorations on some gingerbread people. Eight baker's dozen on a prepaid special order due to be picked up in the morning.

Reiver knelt and sorted through the remains of the torn boxes. "Not a single crumb left behind."

"What I don't get is, why they didn't they just steal

the boxes? Why take the cookies out at all?"

A faint shriek drew their attention to the front of the store. They were both moving by the time they heard the breaking glass.

As they hit the road, both Leif and Reiver stumbled to a halt at the scene before them.

A woman in Christmas-tree-patterned fleece leggings, an oversized knit sweater, and socks over her calves danced in the snowy road, dodging what appeared to be a giant gingerbread monster. It held a lawn stake with a glowing snowman on the end and threatened the woman, who lacked a weapon of her own. She resorted to grabbing loose snow from the road and flinging it, to no effect.

"What is that?" Reiver exclaimed, angling to the left, knowing Leif would head for the right.

"Gingerbread man."

Reiver cleared his throat. "Um, seriously?"

"It appears someone's animated your wife's baked goods." The why didn't matter for the moment. Stopping the gingerbread did.

The woman had realized her pathetic snowballs wouldn't be enough. She saw him and yelled, "Watch out. The cookie attacks."

"Stand aside. I've got this." Leif pulled a pair of specially crafted candy canes from the holsters by his hips and charged them with a bit of Christmas magic. Their red-and-white length swirled, taking on a bright greenish blue glow. With them held upright, Leif confronted the monstrous-sized gingerbread man.

The good news about animated cookies? Easy to break into pieces. More annoying? When those pieces kept trying to rejoin instead of dying.

Leif spun and swung his rods, breaking off a gingerbread limb before shifting to aim for the arm. By the time he'd chopped it off, the leg had reattached. He'd never seen the like.

Reiver growled, "How do we stop it?"

"I don't know." Cookies usually crumbled and stayed that way.

A sharp whistle whipped Leif's head to the side. Mindy stood in the mouth of the alley by the bakery, a green glow surrounding her, even thicker around her rounding belly. She pointed to the monster already reassembling and said, "Mungo, tell your friends it's snack time."

A wave of green-skinned creatures poured out of the alley, led by one wearing a bright purple sarong with a scar over its eye screaming, "Follow."

The goblins swarmed the cookie monster, but rather than tear it apart with their claws, they chomped with their teeth. In under a minute, the locust-like scavengers had eaten every single last morsel, shattering the magic.

The threat was gone.

The woman it had attacked sat in the road, a stunned expression on her face.

Leif knelt by her side. "Ma'am, are you okay?"

She blinked at him from behind her glasses before saying, "Holy baby in a manager, you have pointed ears."

CHAPTER
SIX

WEARING GREEN UNDERWEAR WITH A BIG RED BOW THAT SAID, "UNWRAP ME..."

BELLA WANTED TO SLAP A HAND OVER HER MOUTH THE MOMENT her comment about pointed ears slipped out. How rude of her to remark on it. She couldn't excuse the fact she'd never seen an elf.

Wait, was he an elf? Her understanding of the species was that they were much shorter, and this fellow holding out his hand to her had many inches over her scant five-foot-two stature. A fact realized as he heaved Bella to her feet.

"Hi," she said. "Sorry about what I said."

"Why apologize? It's true. My ears are pointed." Rather than appear offended, Leif grinned and his eyes twinkled with mirth. His smile sparkled with goodwill. His coat might be long and somber, but those weapons he'd wielded...no mistaking their candy cane style.

"Who are you?" she asked.

"Someone wondering why that cookie monster was trying to kill you."

The reminder had her frowning and glancing to her store. "Inside, when it was a single small cookie, it asked me to give it."

"Give it what?" he asked in a low tone.

"I haven't the slightest clue. But it stopped asking after it turned into mega cookie. Then it just wanted to kill me." Her nose wrinkled. "As if I needed another reason to dislike gingerbread."

"They might not be the best cookie, but they can be tasty. Better than dry sugar cookies."

"What?" Bella ogled him. "How are you eating them that they're dry? They're meant to be dipped."

"Not practical when I'm in the field. I need cookies I can grab and eat on the go."

"In that case, you should be carrying around fruitcake. I find a high protein one, chock full of nuts, with a bit of coconut and candied fruits, is the most satisfying."

He stared at her oddly for a moment. "I love fruitcake."

She beamed as she exclaimed, "So do I!" Not something that happened often. Most people treated it as if it were the naughty child in the Christmas treat mix. But she liked nothing more than a good fruitcake made with molasses, crunching with every bite.

While she craved a slice, the man with the candy cane rods sheathed them and crouched to listen to a goblin wearing a dress.

She did her best to not squeal. That scary movie she'd seen claimed goblins originated from bad elves. Possible given their pointed ears, but their size and appearance held nothing else in common.

The wave of green bodies fled the road back to the alley, leaving behind the woman with bobbed dark hair and a rounded belly, accompanied by a man armed with a sword, wearing plaid pajama bottoms and black tee. Bella recognized them both as her neighbors. Nice people. Reiver and Mindy. Her an Earth Witch and him a former CA agent. Both excellent bakers. It was a wonder they remained fit.

"...had things perfectly under control," Reiver argued as they neared.

"Under control. Ha! I saw you hacking to no avail. It was like watching a remake of *Fantasia* with my cookies," Mindy scoffed. "Speaking of which, I'll have to call the client and give them a refund since there is no way I'll get another massive batch baked and decorated before pickup."

"That was your cookies? If I'd have known, I might have had a bite." Bella laughed, as did the man who'd rejoined her.

"I thought they weren't your favorite," he murmured.

"Eating a cookie trying to kill me actually sounds delicious."

That caused him to chuckle. "Any idea how they come to life?" He aimed his question at Mindy.

"They weren't when I was icing them."

"Could you have accidentally poured some Earth magic into them when baking?" he further queried.

"Nope."

"Maybe you didn't notice because of the hormones." Reiver palmed her belly and got an elbow.

Mindy huffed. "I am perfectly in control, not to mention I specialize in edible hexes. For more than a few decades now, and I've never had any of my baked goods come to life."

Bella cleared her throat before saying. "I don't think it was you. I saw someone outside your shop just before the window broke."

The remark had Reiver focusing on her. "What did they look like?"

"Like someone hiding under a cloak. Sorry, I know that's not useful," Bella apologized.

"Height? Perhaps they had wide shoulders?" the candy cane man asked.

"Again, sorry, it was really hard to discern details. They did seem to be hunched over. And they definitely stopped in front of your shop."

"Then what did they do?"

Bella shrugged. "No idea. I looked away for a minute, and when I glanced back, the glass was broken and they were gone."

"Someone cast a spell," mused her candy cane rescuer. "You said they broke in as single cookies. When did they turn into the giant one?"

Despite the fact they tried to kill her, she eyed her toes as she mumbled, "It happened after I crushed them. And before you think I'm a murderer, they attacked me and my cat. I didn't know they'd be so easy to break."

His brows almost escaped his face, but it was Mindy who exclaimed, "My cookies attacked?"

"Yeah. Which reminds me, if you're missing some utensils, they're in my shop. I can get them for you."

"Actually, if you don't mind, may I look inside?" Reiver asked.

"Sure. Although you'll have to go through the window." Bella's nose wrinkled. "I never did get a chance to unlock the door to escape."

Reiver entered first, and Mindy waited until he opened the door before she disappeared within, leaving Bella alone with the pointed-ear man, who had more questions.

"Seems to me someone intentionally sent those cookies after you."

"Why would anyone do that?"

He directed his gaze past Bella to her shop. "You sell Christmas items."

"Yes. You think they were trying to rob me? Not exactly the brightest idea. I mean some of my stuff might have high price tags, but they're very specialized items. It takes the right buyer, and that's not always easy to find."

"Could be they went there looking for something specific. You said one of them demanded you give them something."

"Yeah, but they never said what. And it's not as if I have anything a cookie would want. I don't carry candy sprinkles, or any food for that matter."

"Must be something else. What does your shop stock?"

"Everything?" she offered with a lift of her shoulders. "I have all kinds of items inside. Some old, some new. None of them currently related to baking."

"Any magical items?"

"Possibly?" her lilted reply. "I don't have magic myself, so I wouldn't know."

"I can help there if you'll allow me."

"Sure. Be my guest." She hugged herself as the cold finally penetrated her shock.

"I'm sorry. How rude of me to keep you in the cold." The man slipped off his jacket and draped it over her shoulders. It engulfed her in warmth and a minty scent. Mmm. "Let's get you inside where it's warm."

Inside wasn't much better given the broken window. It was Reiver who said, "Seems like the cookies had just started snooping around when they were disturbed."

Mindy clutched the utensils they'd brandished. "I'm so sorry my cookies tried to hurt you."

"Goodness, it's not your fault!" Bella exclaimed.

"Think this might be related to what we were discussing earlier?" Reiver asked the man who'd loaned Bella his coat.

"Seems mighty coincidental considering the only other living cookies I've known originate from my village." The man pursed his lips as he surveyed the shop.

It led to Bella asking, "Who are you?"

Reiver flung an arm around the man with the pointed ears and said, "This is Leif. An old friend of mine from

Cryptid Training School. Leif, this is Bella, our newest neighbor."

"You're a Cryptid Authority agent?" Bella asked.

Mindy giggled. "Not exactly. He's way more interesting than that."

"Hey!" Reiver complained.

Mindy patted his arm. "Don't worry. You're all the fascination I need." The big man appeared somewhat mollified.

Leif held out his hand. "I guess we were never properly introduced. Leif Blitzen."

"Bella Rinkeli." She slid her fingers into his and got a tingle that parted her lips.

His lips quirked. "Nice to meet you, Bella."

"In town visiting for the holidays?" she asked.

"Actually, I'm here from the North Pole on a mission," he confided.

Given her line of work, it was natural for Bella to tease. "Don't tell me you work for Santa Claus."

Leif winked. "In a sense I do. I'm part of the Yule Squad, and I've been sent here to save Christmas."

CHAPTER
SEVEN

ON THE SIXTH DAY OF CHRISTMAS, LEIF PUT HIS FOOT IN HIS MOUTH...

Leif blurted out his objective, and the woman's eyes widened. But she didn't laugh.

Bella did, however, cock her head and say, "Are you an elf?"

He nodded but didn't elaborate. With the excitement of the fight over, he had a chance to finally look at Bella, the clumsy woman of earlier. She wore comfortable clothing patterned in a Christmas theme covering generous curves. Her hair hung over her shoulders in a messy wave with a hint of curl at the bottom.

She looked up at him, her eyes bright behind her glasses as she questioned him further. "Are you from the North Pole? Santa's Village?"

"Yes."

She chewed her full, plump lower lip. "How do I know you're not lying?"

"Elves can't lie. We're banned from Santa's Village if we're caught fibbing." It didn't happen often, but even in one of the top ten happiest places on Earth—they currently ranked behind a temple that offered visitors baby goats in pajamas—discontent could happen. Sometimes greed crept in. Those elves never ended up staying. And once they broke the rules, they could never return.

"How do I know you're not a banned elf lying to me now?"

He couldn't help his laughter. "I'm afraid I can't prove it. But if you ask Reiver, he'll vouch for me."

A dimple appeared in her cheek as she smiled. "Even if you aren't, I appreciate your Christmas spirit." She took a moment to eye him. "Nice buckle." She pointed out the overly large belt adornment with its bright green tree.

He almost wished he had a book to hold in front of him as he managed to say, "Thanks."

Thankfully, she didn't stare for long. She pushed up her glasses as she gazed at him. "You said something about needing help. What can I do?"

"If you don't mind, I'd like to poke around inside your shop. You see, living gingerbread are rare outside of Santa's Village. And the few we get are usually accidental. So, to see them here, a gang seemingly with a task, makes me wonder what they were after and if it's part of my mission to save Christmas."

"You think one of my ornaments is cursed?" Her eyes widened behind her lenses.

What he thought was he might finally have caught a break on his quest. Could Krampus have been the one animating gingerbread with his magic to act as minions? "Let's have a look and find out."

She led the way inside, peeling off her snowy socks as she entered, showing off toes painted in alternating red and green. Inside her shop smelled like home: pinecone, holly berry, and cinnamon. All fragrances he'd grown up with. Shelves lined the walls with village displays and figurines. Tables around the shop held other Christmas items. Racks hung with sweaters and shirts. Bins with wrapping paper. Even spools with ribbon, the fabric, not plastic kind.

A few items lay on the floor, some of them broken. He pointed. "The attack began inside?"

She nodded. "I was upstairs when I heard the bell for the mail slot in my shop ring."

"Was this before or after the cloaked figure and broken window in the bakery?"

"Right after. I thought it might be a squirrel or something that got through the mail slot, only it turned out to be a bunch of those gingerbread cookies carrying forks, spoons, and knives."

"I still can't believe they were armed." While mischievous, usually the animated cookies didn't resort to violence.

She lifted her legging enough to show red marks on her ankles. "Once they attacked, I had no choice but to defend myself. While I was upstairs fetching a dustpan to clean up the mess, the broken pieces turned into mega cookie monster."

Again, not something he'd ever heard of. He moved

around the shop touching things, feeling faint hints of magic, nothing that stood out. While he did that, the woman grabbed a pair of cozy-looking slipper socks from a rack and pulled them on her feet with a sigh.

"Is this everything you have?" he asked.

"There's more in the back room." She pointed.

Before he could check it out, Reiver and Mindy emerged from the back room.

Reiver jerked a thumb over his shoulder. "Nothing on this floor. I can't check the upstairs. Your giant kitty won't let me pass."

"Big Fluff can be territorial," Bella explained.

"I love that name." Mindy giggled.

"Was that horde of goblins yours?" Bella asked in return.

"Not exactly. Their leader, Mungo, is a close friend of mine. The others live in my dumpster."

"There were so many."

Mindy rolled her shoulders. "Yeah, apparently word got around we offer the best leftovers."

"They're not dangerous?"

"Only to their enemies."

"I wonder if I should start leaving treats in mine," Bella mused aloud.

Leif circled the room, hands outstretched, face intense with concentration. A green glow circled him.

It was Mindy who remarked, "I didn't know elven magic was Earth based."

Leif didn't look back as he replied. "All Christmas magic is." Then because even he recognized the answer as too simple, he explained. "It used to be humanity celebrated the winter solstice. Some called it Yuletide. Over time, that celebration evolved and was absorbed into religion and given an unchanging date of December 25th. Since the Earth Mother quite loved Santa and his giving, she used her magic to create us as helpers."

"So, technically, you're an Earth's witch, too." Mindy's conclusion.

"Of a sort. Elves have access to magic, but not the kind you have that is connected to living plants."

"Not just plants. I can magic my cooking, too." Mindy waggled her fingers.

"Which comes from plants. Elven power involves the inanimate. We can manipulate the elements of Earth." Shaping and building was their specialty.

"Wow, I never knew. This is all kinds of awesome." Bella clasped her hands, and her expression shone with enjoyment.

"Indeed, it is," Mindy agreed.

Reiver joined Leif in circling the room, doing his best to examine every single item. And there were many. Leif admired the eclectic array of decorations, some obviously handmade and quite exquisite. But like Reiver, he found nothing out of the ordinary.

Reiver stopped his examination to state, "I've got a sheet of plywood in the basement I can use to cover your window. I'll be back with it right after I see Mindy back to bed."

"I'll go to bed when I'm ready," was Mindy's tart reply. She eyed Bella. "Want me to stick around?"

"No. I'll be fine. That is if you don't mind me accepting Reiver's offer of a covering for the window."

"Keep him and Leif as long as you need," Mindy graciously offered. "And I should warn you, husband, before you smother me with love and get smacked for it, I'm going to reheat that pizza in the fridge."

Reiver grinned. "Meaning don't expect a piece."

"Baby is hungry." Mindy rubbed her belly.

"Do you need a hand getting the plywood?" Leif asked, eyeing Bella, who was picking up the broken ornaments.

"Nah. I got this. If I need extra hands, Mungo and the gang will help. Although maybe check the doors and windows—even the alley—just in case we missed some cookies."

A good idea. Having not found anything inside the store that screamed evil didn't mean it didn't linger, waiting for another opportunity.

The door to the alley remained barricaded, and a sweep of it showed nothing but a dumpster full of packaging and carboard neatly tied and stacked beside it.

When he returned into the shop, locking the alley door once more, he found Bella sweeping the floor, her back to him. He paused and couldn't have said why the sight of her filled him with...joy.

Joy for someone he'd literally just met. How strange.

The return of Reiver, carrying the plywood while a green army of goblins handled the tools, shattered his contemplation. Together they quickly installed the plywood over the broken window. When done, Reiver asked Bella, "Need anything else? Did Leif check upstairs?"

"Oh, that's not necessary," Bella quickly exclaimed.

"I'm going to check it out," Leif firmly stated.

"Want help?" Reiver offered, but Leif shook his head.

"I've got this. Go to sleep. I know you've got an early morning." While technically still early at just past ten, he knew his friend got up before dawn to start his baking.

As Reiver took his leave, Bella murmured softly, "You really didn't have to stay, but at the same time I do appreciate it."

"It's my pleasure." It really was.

"Shall we go upstairs?"

At his nod, she first locked the shop door then led the way. On their ascent, they had to pause, as a massive, long-haired cat sat on a step, blocking their path. It eyed him with a twitch of its whiskers.

"It's okay, Big Fluff. He's a good guy."

He could have stated all of Santa's elves were required to be good guys, but he basked in the praise instead.

The cat turned and led the way, meowing at the door at the top, and then they walked inside a cozy apartment, the kind that invited a person to come in, sit down, and relax. A plaid couch took up the most room and held a knitted afghan over the back. A rocking chair sat angled to the fireplace with fat cushions for the seat and back. There was a knotted rag rug under a wooden table. A potted pine tree held white lights and an eclectic array of decorations, most handmade. Some, like the snowman with the lopsided features, obviously created by a child.

He felt instantly at home.

While Bella fed the feline, Leif prowled the space. He did a circuit of the living room, noting the stack of books, some of which he had on his own nightstand, neglected given he'd not been home much since Krampus escaped.

A door off the living area led to a bathroom smelling of her. Cinnamon and nutmeg. His favorite scents.

He poked his head into her bedroom next. The sight of the plush, red plaid comforter atop the sleigh bed had him wanting to crawl in. When he emerged after checking her closet for a cookie intruder, she eyed him from the kitchenette.

"Did you find anything?" she asked.

"No. The place is clear. Didn't sense any signs of strong magic either. Could it be something you purchased for the store? Are you expecting any shipments?"

She shook her head. "Not this close to Christmas. Last thing I got was my present from Mom."

At the word present, he approached the tree and ran his hand up and down, looking for a tingle. There was magic here, that of love and, oddly, protection. A pattern repeated, he realized, as he explored her apartment. The afghan oozed comfort. The dream catcher in the window whispered privacy.

He whirled on Bella. "I thought you didn't do magic?"

"I don't."

"Then how is it you're surrounded by hints of it?" he asked, waving his hand.

"I'm not."

"You are," he insisted. "This blanket, your rug, even that shawl you just draped around your shoulders, they all have smidges of magic."

"The only thing they have in common is my mom made them." She hugged the fabric around her upper body. "And I'm pretty sure I'd know if she was a witch."

"Maybe she never told you."

"I don't see why she'd lie."

"It's not a lie if it's an omission," he stated. A fine point he well knew since none of the elves in Santa's Village could fib.

"I don't think I like your implication." She frowned, and it bothered him. He much preferred her smiling.

"It's possible she might not have told you to protect you. Or it could be she's been doing magic unconsciously. What I do know, is this many defensive charms indicates to me she's worried about your safety."

"Why would anyone hurt me?" She sounded quite incredulous.

"Because you love Christmas," he replied grimly. "There are some who would see any signs of joy eradicated from the world."

"Bunch of grinches," she grumbled.

That made him smile. "Indeed." He pivoted but could sense nothing tugging at him. Meaning he had no reason to stay. His glance fell on a crate on her table and slid away.

With a frown, he brought his gaze back and forced himself to stare until beads of sweat popped out on his forehead. He managed, through a gritted jaw, to say, "What's in the box?"

"Present from Mom."

"I need you to open it."

"Excuse me? I don't think so. Mom told me to wait for her."

"There's something in that box."

"A present. I know." She rolled her eyes.

"I mean something that doesn't want to be seen."

That caused her to snort. "Because it's a surprise."

"I'm opening the box."

She threw herself in front of it. "Oh no you're not."

"I'm afraid you have no choice. This is a matter of Holiday Security." He grabbed her by the upper arms and felt a tingle strong enough he froze.

She stilled.

Their eyes locked.

A frozen moment in time.

Interrupted by a cat horking up a hairball.

Bella glanced away and ducked her head, unable to hide her red cheeks. "I don't see why you need to open a gift from my mom. I can assure you it's not some kind of weapon or bomb."

"I'll be the judge of that." He couldn't help thinking of what he and Reiver had spoken of. How Krampus might be contagious. What if Santa hadn't escaped that pit but the thing that made Krampus had? What if this box—

He ceased that line of thought because it was absurd. Even if Krampus could be boxed and mailed, why would Bella's mom send it to her?

Before he could apologize, Bella's chin lifted. "I'm sorry, but if you want to open that box, I'm going to need some kind of warrant. I mean you don't even work for the CA, so what gives you the authority to make demands?"

"I am invested by the authority given to me as a Yule Squad member on a mission direct from Candy Cane Central, which is—"

"Cute, and possibly delusional, but isn't going to change my mind, especially as I'm having doubts you're an elf from the North Pole."

"Reiver can vouch for me."

"He's your friend. Of course he would."

"What will it take to convince you?" he asked on a sigh.

"If you want me to disobey my mother and open that box, then I'll need more than just your word. Surely you can prove what you say."

"Time is of the essence. And I apologize if this is strange to you, but these are unprecedented times. Christmas itself is at stake."

"Why is it in danger?"

Rather than lie, he stuck to omission. "It's a matter of holiday security."

She snorted. "Says you."

"Elves can't lie."

"If you're an elf. According to everything I know about the North Pole, you're too tall to be who you say."

He winced. "Wow, that was uncalled for."

Her lips turned down. "You're right. That was rude. Sorry. However, see it from my perspective. It's always been my understanding that, apart from Buddy in that movie, the elves in Santa's Village are under four feet in height."

"Mostly true. We have some that are taller."

"Like you?"

"I'm what you call a mixed breed. Only half elf."

"What's the other half?" she asked.

Since he couldn't lie… "Reindeer."

She blinked. "As in four legs and a rack?"

"When shifted, yes. And before you ask, the village also has a few snowcats, yetis, and even some humans."

"You forgot Santa." Her sarcastic reminder.

He pursed his lips, afraid he'd admit something the world wasn't ready for. He did say, "I wish I could tell you more."

"Rather than tell, why not show me some proof?"

"Show you? I don't have time. It's only days until Christmas."

"And? You're a reindeer, right? Doesn't Santa travel the whole world in one night delivering toys with his reindeer?"

"Christmas was—is—special." Back in the day, when Santa held the reins, his dad spoke of how they flew faster than normal.

"Asking me to believe yet offering excuses." She shook her head.

There was one way of getting there fast. If one didn't mind being turned inside out and possibly disappearing forever. He'd done it only twice. Swore never again.

But as he'd said to her just moments before, extenuating circumstances applied and they had little time. He thought of shifting but was oddly shy about stripping in front of her.

"Would seeing Santa's Village convince you?"

"Is this where you lure me to your car, drive us somewhere remote, and kill me?"

He blinked. "No."

"Then how will we get there?"

"Just hold on to me and don't let go." He held out his hand, asking her to trust.

The moment she laced her fingers with his, once more shocking him at the touch, it hit him; he could hold it forever.

It caused his heart to freeze in his chest. His mouth to turn dry.

She obviously wasn't as affected, as she said, "Now what happens?"

"Now we ask for a portal." He pressed the engraved tree on his belt buckle.

A voice replied, saying, "Hey, Blitzen. What's up?"

"I need a portal for two."

"Really?" Such surprise in that one word. "Right away. Stand by in three, two, one."

A swirling morass of red, green, and white appeared

in Bella's living room, bringing a hint of ice and sending her cat yowling into the bedroom.

A slack-jawed Bella stared.

He tugged her toward it. "We need to step through."

"Is that safe?"

"Mostly." So long as they didn't hear voices, they should make it to the other side.

"Where does it go?"

"You'll see. You wanted proof. This is the only way we can do so quickly. But bring that package with us just in case it's important. Wouldn't want it to get into the wrong hands."

She snared the box one armed, never loosening her grip. Rather it tightened as they stepped into the portal together and emerged in the North Pole under an arch by the massive outdoor Christmas tree.

As she gaped with jaw-dropped astonishment, he said, "Welcome to Santa's Village."

CHAPTER

EIGHT

WISHING SHE'D CHANGED INTO HER BEST
CHRISTMAS DRESS WITH LIGHTS THAT
BLINKED ON AND OFF ...

BELLA HONESTLY DIDN'T EXPECT LEIF TO TAKE HER ANYWHERE. She'd meant to call his bluff. After all, despite loving Christmas and her mother insisting Santa and the elves were real, she'd been raised in the age of the internet. She knew fact from fiction, even as she humored her mother. After all, some people believed in one God, some sacrificed to Satan, others worshipped the Earth Mother. If given a choice, why not believe in Christmas?

But loving the Yuletide didn't mean she'd immediately believe a guy claiming to be an elf from the North Pole. Pointed ears? Surgery. Candy cane weapons? Cool. But anyone could special order those. All the things he claimed? Could be fiction. However, even she had nothing left to argue when Leif conjured a portal and they emerged somewhere built of ice and snow with cozy cottages—the kind often seen in the older European areas—with thick thatched roofs and solid log and stone construction. The trim on them was ornate and brightly colored in the primaries: red, blue, yellow, and green with lots of white.

The bustling figures ranged in height from barely knee high to a hairy eight feet tall at least. Even more incongruous, the shaggy yeti wore a striped poncho.

"Um." She lacked the ability to speak.

"I'm sorry? I didn't hear that. Could you repeat?" Leif asked with a bright twinkle in his eye.

"Tinsel on a tree, you told the truth. You really are an elf from Santa's Village."

"Told you. I can't lie." He'd earned his smug pleasure.

"Guess I should apologize for ever doubting you were one of Santa's elves."

Which led to a snort from her left. "Him, an elf? Ha! Takes more after his mother, he does."

A glance showed a stocky person, not quite waist high, with pronounced pointed ears and a most impressive nose, walking past them toward one of the adorable buildings.

"That was a real elf?"

"As opposed to me?" He said it mockingly.

"I'm sorry. I wasn't meaning to be rude."

"It's not rude because you're right. I'm only part elf. The other half is reindeer from my mom's side.

"Meaning your dad was an elf?" Then before she could stop herself, she blurted out, "How does that work?"

His lips stretched as he drawled, "When two people really like each other—"

Her blush threatened to ignite her face. She turned

and started talking to avoid her embarrassment. "We appear to have landed in some kind of park." Or so it appeared, given the lovely, patterned ice pavers underfoot and the sculptures inside bright planters. Benches were set up so villagers could enjoy the massive living tree adorned in ornaments. "It's beautiful."

"Thanks. You can see my contribution up there." He pointed up high. "Every elf creates at least one and then choses a spot for it."

"What did you make?"

"I fabricated a miniature skateboard. At the time, I was obsessed with them."

"So it's true. Santa's elves make toys and other things."

"We used to when the toys were just wood and fabric, but once those items became commercialized and mostly made of plastic, we had to come up with new methods that automated much of the process."

"Is that a fancy way of saying you use a factory?"

"Yep, but not one manned by machines, but elves working in tandem, each with a specific task suited to their magical skill."

"Meaning what exactly?"

"For example, a friend of mine, Sloopy, is really good when it comes to shaping the rubber and plastic to make limbs, bodies and heads for dolls, but terrible at creating hair, faces and clothes. So, when he's done shaping, he hands to an elf who's good at that kind of stuff."

"Making each toy a group effort."

"Exactly." He pointed up the road. "About a mile

from here is Plum Pudding Factory and, beside it, the newer Eggnog Electronics."

"I'd ask if you were joking, but I do believe you'd prove me wrong." She shook her head as her worldview expanded. "What are the other buildings?"

The village was more than a few structures. It sprawled with streets and intersections. No cars, although she did see some carts being pulled by a variety of animals, including a team of penguins in bright red bow ties who hooted as they sped past a stalled carriage, whose harnessed bear chose to have a nap despite the hand waving of the woman haranguing it.

"The tower you see over there is Candy Cane Central." He indicated a tall building that reminded her of a lighthouse given its skinny height and what appeared to be windows ringing the very top. "Most of the day-to-day stuff is handled in there. One street over from it is the Gingerbread Sweets Emporium. By the east gate we have the Jingle Bell Barn, which is where I work. In front of us is the library." He offered an indication of his head to the pyramid of glass.

Even from where they stood, she could see hammocks hung in various spots spanning the window. What a lovely place to curl up.

A building with fragrant aromas had her exclaiming, "That smells like a restaurant."

"Because it is. There are some all over offering various cuisines. For those who prefer to cook and eat at home, we also have bakeries, butchers, and supply stores."

"Like a real town," she murmured. "What currency do you use?"

"None. No one pays for anything here."

"Then how does the restaurant operate?"

His lips lifted at the corners. "It makes food. People eat it."

"But how do they buy the food and pay those working?"

"There is no money here. The gardeners grow produce in the greenhouses and give it to the restaurants and food shops. People take what they need. They cook. They share."

The concept was beautiful. "It sounds lovely."

"For us, yes, but I'll admit, it's not a concept that has worked well outside the village."

"Humanity would have issues." Not everyone wanted to work. She scrunched her nose. "I love the idea of being able to sit down to food and not worry about the making of it. Who does the dishes?"

"Dishwasher, of course. Did you think we only built toys?" he teased.

"I don't know what to think anymore." The honest truth. She eyed more buildings, some taller and larger than others.

He answered before she asked. "Those big structures are the apartment complexes: Mistletoe, Chestnut, Glitter..." He named off more than expected.

"How many people live here?"

"As many as it takes to keep Santa's Village running and ensure good children get their gifts."

"This place is huge and, by the sounds of it, a well-oiled machine. Why do you think it's in trouble?"

"The threat isn't to the village specifically, but to Christmas."

"And you thought that threat might be something in my shop? Or in this box?" She gave it a jiggle.

"The issue is we don't know what we're looking for other than the threat is an ancient one."

"Please don't say it's Krampus." She hugged herself as a shudder went through her.

"You know the stories." A grimly spoken reply that did not help.

"I've heard a few things. None of them good." She'd never had interest in a monster doing violence at Christmas.

He glanced away and appeared to be mulling something before saying, "Krampus has escaped his prison."

"Oh no!" She didn't have to fake dismay.

"We need to find him before he hurts anyone. The problem is we don't know where he's hiding."

"I think I would have noticed a hoofed and horned murderer in the neighborhood."

"Krampus wears a human face, and the horns aren't always in evidence."

"Any face? Or does he stick to one in particular?"

"It's changed over the years," he hedged.

"Whose face does he currently have?" His very reluctance indicated the importance.

"Older man, possibly rotund around the middle, white beard, like to wear red and white—"

"It almost sounds like you're describing Santa." At the way his lips turned down, she gasped. "Wait, you're telling me Krampus is Santa Claus?"

He winced and put a finger to his lips. "Not so loud. We're trying to keep it under wraps for the moment to avoid any panic."

Too late, her heart fluttered rapidly. "I don't understand."

"Neither do we. There's a gap in our knowledge when it comes to Krampus and how he came into being. Near as I've been able to figure out, it appears Krampus possessed Santa and rather than kill him, we placed him in a prison."

"Santa's in jail?" This time she remembered to whisper her shock.

"Not anymore. We think. We aren't actually sure what happened to him. All we know is Krampus most definitely escaped, which is a bad thing—"

"Because he kills people," she interrupted. "Wow. Oh wow." She felt lightheaded. "I need to sit down."

He guided her to a bench. "I'm sorry."

"Don't apologize. I asked. Not your fault the truth took me by surprise." She set the crate from her mom in her lap. She stared at it then him. "Could Krampus have sent those gingerbread to my store?" Because he'd implied the animation of them was a magic he knew of.

"I'd say it's very possible."

"If that's true, then he sent them because he's looking for something. Something holiday themed given they raided my shop. When he was imprisoned, where did his belongings go? Was he stripped and sent in naked? Could he be seeking a particular artifact?" Bella had seen a poster once of yet another Christmas Krampus-themed horror movie where he held some looped chains.

"I don't know the answer to any of those questions." Leif shrugged. He hastened to add, "There's very little information about Krampus in our archives. I mean I've heard stories and seen paintings of battles between Santa and the monster where Santa wins. But the most recent encounter is lacking in detail. All we know is Santa turned into Krampus, started killing, but hid it for a while until the elves caught on. He was captured and put in a deep prison shaft layered in spells where he should have been unable to escape."

"But did."

"We think he had help."

"Who would help a killer monster?" she exclaimed.

"That's what I said!" Leif gestured. "Not to mention they did so at the worst possible time."

"Is he already killing?" she asked, her eyes wide in shock.

"We can't tell. It's not that easy anymore to filter Krampus crime from the usual."

"The world needs a little more goodwill." She ducked her head. "What are you going to do when you find him?"

"I don't know. Call it in and let the Musher and others in charge handle it."

"I hear a but," she prodded.

It took Leif a moment to gather his thoughts and express them. "Will they know how to deal with him? I kind of have to wonder because no one I asked remembers how they did it. They all say the same thing: we got rid of his magic and put him in prison."

"Hearing yet another but."

"My mind keeps coming back to a niggling point. Santa, even infected, had a lot of magic, much more than an elf or a witch. It was how he lived for so long. How he created everything about Christmas." Leif's hands gestured to encompass the space around them. "He could even fly."

"And?"

"The only reason that prison held Santa was because they took his magic."

"Who did?"

He shrugged. "No one seems to remember."

"That seems strange."

"I would have said suspicious, actually."

Her eyes widened. "Do you think they might have placed the magic inside something?"

He nodded. "It would make sense. Would even explain why those cookies came to your shop."

"Because what better spot to hide Santa's magic than inside something Christmas-y. But how would it end up in my store? Wouldn't an object that important be guarded?"

"Only if the person who had it remembered," he countered.

"Meaning Santa's magic could be inside anything."

She eyed the crate in her lap. "I don't suppose you can grope it and see if it's magic without opening it?"

"Sorry. The box is shielded. I can't sense anything inside."

"Oh." Her shoulders slumped, because, while she hated disobeying her mom, this was more important than a secret meant for Christmas morning.

Leif cleared his throat. "I have an idea. Turn your back while I look. If you don't see it, it doesn't count as opening."

He had a point.

"Do it quick before I change my mind." She offered him her back and then had to fight to not squirm as she heard the creak of the wooden lid being removed, the rustle of straw. His apology as he said, "It's wrapped." The crinkle of paper as he opened her present.

Then nothing.

She waited, struggling with the urge to turn her head and look.

Eventually she heard reverses of the rustles and creaks as he repackaged it and said, "No magic."

"You're sure it's not related to the Krampus situation?"

"Very." And that was all he said. Not even a clue as to what he'd seen. It burned her he knew and she didn't. Christmas was so far away!

"It's safe to look again," he said softly.

She eyed the package a little too eagerly as if hoping he'd missed a spot and she'd get a peek.

The box sat there looking how it began. Mysterious. And not the clue he'd been hoping for.

"Guess those cookies were wrong."

"Maybe." He didn't sound certain. "You hungry?"

Despite the time of night, her stomach replied with a startlingly loud gurgle.

He laughed and held out his hand. "Come on. I know a place that does the best turkey leftovers for those who stay up late. I hope you like frothy potatoes, cranberry sauce, and the best gravy."

"That's like my favorite food."

"Me, too." He held out his hand, and she took it without hesitation.

As she followed the elf to the restaurant across the square, an odd thought crossed her mind.

Do elves date humans?

CHAPTER
NINE

THINKING MAYBE HE SHOULD BE WEARING THE SHIRT THAT SAID MERRY DRUNK, I'M CHRISTMAS...

SOMETHING WAS WRONG WITH LEIF.

He'd first suspected it when he'd made the snap decision to bring Bella to the North Pole. A choice that made no sense. Of all things he could have done to prove his identity—shifting into his reindeer shape, creating a toy using magic and mundane items—he'd chosen instead to bring her to the village.

The top-secret, hidden, no-one-could-ever-know-its location Santa's Village.

Sure, the portal wasn't exactly a map to its location, and yet, by showing a human it truly existed, he'd invited possible future problems. What if she told people about it? What if they believed her? What if he'd made a grave mistake?

And what was he thinking using a portal? He'd guaranteed a return trip.

Then again, all that faded in the face of Bella's pleasure as she admired Santa's Village. Why did he care what she thought? He had no need to prove himself to her. Leif had a mission. One he could have accomplished by hexing her into sleep. A simple magic all elves knew given their ancestors used it often once upon a time when they aided Santa in delivering gifts. A few light sleeping children had caused chaos, so they'd learned to ensure a household slumbered before they went to work.

But instead of putting Bella to sleep and checking the package she so insistently refused, he'd taken her home.

And people noticed.

His elongated ears caught the snippets of conversation

"Who is she?"

"Figures he'd choose a human."

"He should be doing his job."

A reminder to not get distracted, which he ignored as he invited her to a late-night dinner, where he sat across from her, watching her groan in enjoyment as she savored a leftover sandwich made from his favorite meal. Hers, too, apparently. He justified his decision with the reminder that Daphne, their reputable seer, had sent him to Reiver, knowing he'd run into Bella, a woman with a Christmas shop attacked by gingerbread people. It had to mean something.

He didn't find out what during dinner, although he did discover she loved roasting chestnuts—him, too— hated scary movies—another ditto—and she lived in service to her cat.

A cat that they'd left behind and was the only reason why he didn't ask her if she'd like to spend the night.

With him.

Because the more time they spent together, the more Leif wanted to kiss her. Among other things. Never mind the fact they'd just met. Everything about her attracted him.

"You're staring at me," she softly chided.

"I was wondering what you'd do if I tried to kiss you."

She arched a brow. "Do you want to kiss me?"

"Yes."

"We just met."

"I know. It's the reason why I'm wondering instead of finding the nearest hanging sprig of mistletoe."

Her lips curved as she confided, "I know where to find some. But it's back at my place."

The invitation took him by surprise, but he wasn't about to say no. "Shall we?"

He hoped he kept their pace to a seemly walk and not an almost-trot. They held hands again, and he almost snapped when someone dared to greet him and he had to waste a few seconds replying.

Hammy, when contacted, wisely didn't question his request for a portal. Not that he needed an excuse. Yet knowing he did so for carnal reasons and not mission ones did nag his guilt.

However, stepping into her home and having her lead him to a sprig of mistletoe just inside her bedroom door had him forgetting everything but his sudden insatiable need for this woman.

Sometimes people confused biblical sins with naughty and nice. Some things were obvious, killing and stealing for gain? Bad. But death to protect, theft to feed or aid someone in need? Good.

Sex between two consenting adults? Also good.

He cupped her face and kissed her. And kept kissing her as they stumbled into her bedroom. He paused the embrace only long enough to ask, "Are you sure?"

"Very." She wrapped her arms around his neck and tugged him close.

The bed was right there, and he guided her to it, helping her with her sweater as she tried to tear it off and got stuck. His jacket hit the floor first. Then his own shirt.

Pants proved just as complicated, as her leggings got tight around her ankles and she toppled on to the bed. He grinned as he untangled her, and she rolled to her back.

"I'm a little clumsy."

"I hadn't noticed," he chuckled. He knelt on the bed and grabbed her ankles, pulling her toward him and parting her thighs, but it was the shape on her hip that intrigued him.

"A tattoo?" He ran his finger over the mark.

"Birthmark, actually."

"It looks like a silver bell."

"If you say so. I've thought about having it removed."

"Don't. It's a part of you." He leaned down to kiss it. A brief brush of his lips and she shivered.

While he wanted to embrace her again, all that inviting skin begged for his touch. He bent and kissed the inside of her thigh, feeling a slight tremor. He slid his mouth up the curve of her hip and stopped only at the edge of her panties. Christmas themed and essentially begging he tug them off.

They hid her entirely, and yet he'd never seen anything sexier. He pressed his face against the material covering her mound, inhaling the sweet scent of her desire. He then blew hotly in the crease between her thighs.

She moaned.

He couldn't resist. With just his teeth, he pulled her panties down. She lifted her hips, allowing him to tug them past the round curve of her ass all the way to her feet. He let them drop to the floor, but before he could return to the treasure he'd unwrapped, he caught her expression. Glasses askew, bottom lip caught with her teeth, skin flushed, and hands gripping her comforter.

"By all the pine needles on the big tree, you are beautiful," he huffed.

She smiled at him. "And you're probably the sexiest thing to come out of the North Pole."

Rather than blush, he returned to the present she'd given him, pink and wet. Delicious. Leif pressed his mouth to her and exulted in her quiver. He licked her and teased her. Found her button of pleasure and played with it until she bucked. He didn't stop, just grabbed hold of her hips and kept on giving.

She moaned and trembled, her hands digging into her blanket. And he kept going, the scent just making him hum. He kept licking as he slid two fingers into her, groaning when she clamped down.

"Merry Christmas to me," he murmured against her as he kept thrusting, faster and faster until she came, her climax gripping his fingers almost painfully tight.

When she loosened, he slid up her body slowly, his mouth exploring as his fingers started circling her clit. She moaned into his mouth as he brought her back to the edge.

Her hands began tugging at his pants.

Yes.

His hands went over hers on the buckle, helping her to detach it. He unbuttoned his jeans next. She grabbed hold of him, and he hissed, almost spilling some fresh nog into her hand.

She kissed him and whispered, "I want you."

Not as desperately as he wanted her. But before he could sink into her and give them what they both needed, his pants, only halfway down his legs, began to ring.

He didn't want to answer. He really, really didn't.

But he couldn't shirk duty for pleasure.

"Nipping frost on my toes, I've got to go." He rose from the bed and filled his senses with the languorous splay of her limbs.

"Now?" Incredulity and disappointment in that one word.

He felt the same way. Passion still raged within. He wanted nothing more than to sink into her warmth, but duty called.

Stridently. The special ring tone could mean only one thing.

"There's an emergency in the village." He offered a hard kiss of regret and whispered, "Might I call upon you again?"

"I'd like that," she said almost shyly as she drew a blanket over her nakedness.

"I'll be back soon," he promised. He grabbed his clothes and dressed as he strode into the living room. An emergency meant he had to return immediately. No time to fly home.

Much as he hated the idea, he'd have to call for another portal. Three in one night!

He slapped his belt buckle. A portal appeared instantly without him even asking.

Must be dire. Hoping his luck with the portal held, he stepped inside, and his entire being lurched unpleasantly.

Erp. While he'd managed to hold his guts the previous two jumps, he lost it this time. He arrived, stumbling into the square, bent over, spasming and nauseous, feeling as if he'd been turned inside out and then spun wildly. He'd rather be drunk on holly-berry wine. It should be noted he hated the sweet stuff.

He heaved in a deep breath then another, taking a few seconds to calm himself and realize he smelled smoke. He lifted his head and took a glance around. People ran around the square. Some hustled children and elderly to homes for safety; others carried buckets or jammed helmets on their heads as they pulled on fireproof coats.

There was no yelling or panic, just stoic determination. Elves just did the job.

A fellow in a bright yellow coat went to pass by, a metal bucket rattling by his thigh. Leif flagged him. "What's happened?"

"Fire!"

Obviously. "Where?"

The location was important when it came to knowing how to combat it. A place with many combustibles would need magic to help contain any shockwaves and flying debris. Actual flames required water, and given the expense to keep pipes flowing in the cold ground, they instead maintained a tanker. Only he knew for a fact it was currently in the shop getting repaired. An axle snapped, mostly likely from disuse. They didn't get many fires because they'd long ago retrofitted homes with fire-retardant materials.

Only a few places hadn't yet been renovated. Only one in the direction of the smoke. And he knew suddenly where the fire burned.

The elf he'd waylaid shouted confirmation as he ran off to help. "It's the mansion."

Leif sprinted after him, passing him and others heading in that direction. He didn't slow to help the bucket brigade soaking the area around the fire in order to save the rest of the village. Leif aimed for the source, a grand house currently aflame, and no amount of thrown water or stifling spells could put it out.

By dawn, Santa's house had burned to the ground.

CHAPTER
TEN

WHILE HER NIGHTIE DECLARING ELF SHENANIGANS REMAINED IN HER DRESSER...

Bella lay in bed, body pleasantly throbbing, bemused by what had just happened. She'd basically had sex with a guy she'd literally met that very same day.

Shocking, only for those that treated intercourse and the foreplay surrounding it as something bad. While her mother had raised her to wait and make it special with "the one," Bella ascribed to a more modern feminine belief that she owned her body, she could satisfy her needs, and if she chose to get emotionally attached, it would be because she saw something in another person that went beyond brief pleasure.

Speaking of brief...

A shame Leif had to leave before finishing. She'd never seen a man's belt buckle light up like that before. For a teensy tiny second, when that Christmas tree on it was glowing and blinking, she'd thought it had something to do with his ardent desire.

He desired her all right, but it wasn't enough to keep

him in her bed. He left her to handle an emergency in the North Pole. Given her line of business, the irony didn't escape her.

Would he come back tonight? He'd said soon. Did he say that because he felt like he had to, given her nakedness at the time? What if he didn't want to come back? Or something happened to him and she never knew!

Ugh.

Mooning over him accomplished nothing. Sleep. Work. Wait and see what happened.

Easier decided than done. It took her forever to drift off, and when she eventually woke, it was to a cat sitting on her chest, glaring.

"Sorry, Big Fluff. I overslept." Indeed, she'd blown well past her usual eight a.m. wakeup, and it was almost ten. The shop was supposed to open soon.

Yikes.

"Meow."

Her feline had been inordinately patient if she'd waited this long to complain.

"My poor baby. You must be starving. Wasting away. Holding on by a thread. Don't worry, my sweet ball of love. Mama will feed you." Don't judge. Big Fluff was her world, especially with Mom travelling so much the last few years.

Once her cat had been fed, Bella rushed around, washing, dressing, and shoving an untoasted Pop-Tart—breakfast of champions!—into her mouth, washed down with a hot chocolate. It wasn't until she entered the gloomy shop at quarter past ten that she remembered the broken window from the night before.

Even having the lights on did little to lighten the room. It felt like a cave. If it weren't so cold outside, she'd have propped open the front door. She flipped the sign to Open then just removed it from the door to let some natural daylight enter.

Before she tackled some of the disarray, she browsed the internet for repair services that could handle a window. The door jangled as someone entered. Bella glanced over to see a woman in clean gray overalls, her hair pulled back in a ponytail, carrying a toolbox. The stranger cleared her throat. "Hi, are you Bella Rinkeli?"

"Yes. Can I help you?" She shoved at her glasses. A miracle they'd survived the previous day. Just in case, she kept a drawer with two other pairs.

"I'm Avery from Big A's Glass and Repair. I was called about a window."

Despite wanting to hug the woman in front of her, as she provided the exact help she needed, Bella did have a question. "Called by who?"

"A friend of mine, Mindy. Owns the bakery across the street. She said you needed your window fixed ASAP and to give you the friends-and-family discount."

"Oh yes, please!" Bella clapped her hands. "It's a Christmas miracle."

Avery chuckled. "If you say so. What happened to the window?"

Bella froze, at a loss what to say because admitting a giant cookie smashed it might send Avery fleeing for a saner client. She settled on, "Rambunctious Christmas revelers."

"Hope they didn't steal much. You've got some cool shit." Avery gave a turn and nod of her head in the direction of the Christmas village laid out over several floating shelves starting waist high and going up. Enough shelf space to create a large town that included a bookstore, a few pubs, churches, stores, all lit up and accessorized. It proved very popular, and she had to refill spots on the shelves daily.

"Thankfully, the damage proved minimal," Bella replied, still unsure what the gingerbread had wanted from her.

"Glad to hear it. Let's get that window fixed up for you."

"Do you need help?" Bella asked.

"Don't worry about me. I'll have someone giving me a hand when it comes time to setting the actual window. First, I've got to measure so I can have the shop trim something down to size. While they do that, I'll prep the opening."

"Sounds good."

"I'll have a quote for you within the hour. But I can tell you right now, we're looking between three and four to replace it."

She winced but nodded. "Do it."

"You can probably run it by your insurance for reimbursement."

"Probably." Bella didn't mention the lack of insurance. Blame Mom. She didn't understand why she should pay a middleman money just so they could hire someone to fix her things. She'd rather just fix them herself.

Avery went out and began prying at the window. Bella quickly cleared everything from the display, placing it all in the back. She'd need to check the items for damage, seeing as how they'd gotten banged around during her tussle with the gingerbread.

While in the back, Bella saw the perfect thank-you for her kind neighbor. She placed it in a little gift bag to carry across the road. She entered the bakery, expecting to see the matronly woman who handled the sales. To her surprise, Mindy sat behind the counter.

Mindy smiled wide at Bella. "Hey, how are you?"

"Thankful for the help you sent over."

"Given you're new to the area, I figured you could use someone reliable, and Avery's service and rates can't be beat."

"Not just that, though, last night, too. I don't know what would have happened if you'd all not arrived to the rescue."

"Bah. You seemed to be handling it pretty well. And besides, you would have done the same."

Bella would have tried to help, but judging by last night, she best served as a distraction. "Don't be so sure. I had no idea what I was doing. I've never had to fight off cookies before."

"Me either. Although I did have to slay some of the undead." Mindy wrinkled her nose.

"I really hope I never have to face that because I don't

know if I could hurt a zombie. I can't hurt things with faces."

"Don't tell me you're the type who puts spiders outside."

"I am."

Mindy guffawed. "Me, too. Drives Reiver and my best friend, Annie, nuts. They say I'm just inviting more back inside."

"I've also been known to give rodents tinsel for their nests, along with cheese. Oh, and we once had a lizard living in our house in New Mexico who loved glitter and lights. I even sewed it a little Santa suit."

"Have you lived in many places?"

"Yes. My mother's business takes her around the world."

"What does she do?"

"Imports and exports."

Mindy blinked. "People actually do that?"

The remark had Bella chuckling. "Mine does. She works in historical artifacts of great value that require extra care being transferred."

"Okay, that sounds really cool."

"I guess. While she was always on the hunt for new and interesting things, I just wanted to spend more than a few years in one place." Making friends wasn't easy when you never knew when to expect the moving trucks to arrive.

"And you chose our town to set down roots?"

"Maybe?" An uncertain note that needed explaining.

"More like I'm trying it out. Nowhere I've been to yet feels right."

"You're looking for a home." Mindy nodded. "I get it. I had a townhouse I used to live in, but Mr. Neighbor went a little crazy and set fire to it. Luckily, I got all my plants out in time, but the place was a disaster. We're living above the shop right now, but it's temporary. We're building a place not far from Annie's farm. I want our child to have somewhere to run and play. Explore and build."

"You're moving?" Figured she'd just connected with someone and they were about to leave.

"Hopefully before this little person comes." Mindy patted her belly. "They're working on the interior right now. Reiver won't let me near it because of paint fumes." Mindy rolled her eyes.

"He seems very overprotective."

"He is, but I don't mind." Mindy grinned. "It's part of how he's coping with the fact he's going to be a dad. He's excited and terrified, and he loves me, so the fact my feet hurt and I have to pee all the time has him feeling as if he's failing me somehow because he's not suffering, so he overcompensates taking care of me."

"And you don't mind?"

"Nah. I know I'm a strong, independent woman. But if he wants to carry heavy stuff, including me, then he can have at it."

Must be nice. Bella never had anyone to fuss over her that much. Mom had taken care of her, and very well, but she also expected Bella to handle her own affairs. From a young age, Mom taught her everything. Cooking. Sewing. Crafts. Reading. Writing. Math. She'd been homeschooled for months and years at a time during her youth. The times she wasn't, she went to school with other kids and learned to socialize. Not an easy thing to do when many called her weird. Bella had her own sense of style and a love for Christmas that tended to alienate people.

Bella thrust out the small gift bag. "For the baby."

"Really?" Mindy clapped her hands. "I know this is where I'm supposed to be polite and say you shouldn't have, but I love presents."

At that, Bella full-belly laughed. "Me, too. Check it out."

Mindy withdrew an ornate picture frame with lettering spelling out, "Baby's First Christmas." The silver shone bright. It better given how long Bella had to scrub the antique found in an old box bought at an auction.

"Oh, this is gorgeous. Thank you."

"You're welcome. Thank you for sending me Avery."

"Bah. That's what friends are for." A casual thing to say and yet Bella glowed. Until Mindy added, "Is Leif still in bed?"

"Uh." She couldn't exactly be mad Mindy thought he might be. After all, he'd obviously not returned to his friends' last night. "He had to leave on urgent business. You know, in the North Pole."

"Oh. I didn't know. I hope everything is all right."

A casual Bella—who hid her fluttery heart rate—asked, "Think he'll be back?"

"I assume so given he left his car behind."

"It's a rental."

"Then maybe not. I'll have to ask Reiver."

"What? No." Bella shook her head.

Mindy's lips quirked. "Are you sure? Maybe I should get you his number."

"Nope. No need. But thanks. I really should get back to my shop." Bella waved as she practically bolted out the door.

Way to be obvious about her interest in Leif. Then again, why not? A modern woman was allowed to pursue anyone she wanted. Leif intrigued Bella. Nothing wrong with wanting to explore that further.

Bella jaywalked across the street back to her house—twice in one day, look at her being bad, Santa would be cross— just as her mom called.

"Who broke the window?"

No point in asking how Mom knew. Some people joked their mothers had eyes in the backs of their heads. Bella's possessed prescience. "I don't know who it was." Technically not a lie.

"What did they take?" An urgent demand.

"Nothing." Also true.

"Are you hurt?"

"Not really." Mostly true. The red marks on her ankles from the forking had mostly faded.

"I think you should go stay elsewhere until I get there."

"Which is tonight, so no point in me renting a room."

"Actually"—her mother drew out the word slowly—"I'm a little caught up in something. I won't be able to see you until Christmas Eve."

"What? Why?" The change in plans surprised.

"I need a little more time with my current project. You've got my credit card. Use it and let me know which hotel you're going to. And make sure you keep the door locked. Don't go out at night."

"Mom, you're going overboard. I'm a grown woman, and what happened isn't a big deal. The window is getting fixed as we speak." Avery appeared to be scraping the outer edges of the frame.

"It is a big deal. What if they come back?"

A possibility that Bella had been trying to not dwell on.

"Would you rather I come to you?" Bella offered. She could close the store a little earlier than usual to make her mom happy. "Tell me where to fly and I'll join you."

"I wish it were that simple, sugar plum." A childhood name her mother rarely used given Bella was almost forty, even if most people pegged her for much younger.

"Is everything all right?"

"Yes. Don't worry about me. How are you? How is business?"

Bella didn't tell her about Leif, the gingerbread men, or the fact she'd visited Santa's Village. "Business is good. I sold that nutcracker set you picked up in Prague."

"Very nice. I've got a bead on a set of nesting figurines, hand painted, mid-nineteenth century."

"Oooh. Can't wait."

"You're not going to stay somewhere else, are you?"

"Don't worry, Mom. I'll be fine. The neighbors across the way are keeping an eye on me."

"The hunter and the witch? I guess that's adequate." A grumble by her mother. "Be safe, sugar plum. I love you."

"Love you, too, Mom. Can't wait to see you."

As they hung up, Bella had to wonder what bothered her mother. She sounded strained. Perhaps the work was getting to be too much? For as much as her mother celebrated Christmas, she'd been around during that time less and less of late. And she was looking older, too. She'd aged in the last decade, her hair going silvery white, fine wrinkles appearing at the corners of her eyes.

Mom wasn't supposed to get old.

Bella spent the rest of the afternoon watching Avery fixing the window while helping her customers. Every time the bell rang, her head jerked up, hoping against hope to see a certain someone.

The only thing she saw was a tow truck removing Leif's car just before dinner.

Upstairs, only her cat awaited her. They shared a tub of ice cream while watching a movie favorite—*Die Hard*, because it wasn't Christmas until she saw Hans Gruber fall off the Nakatomi Tower. If her mom were here, they'd have had their yearly argument about whether or not it was a holiday classic. It would end with Mom shaking her head and grumbling, "Just like your father." A man that Mom missed so much that she kept no pictures, nothing. Just dropped the occasional tidbit. He loved cookies. Warm glasses of milk. And Christmas.

By the time Bella crawled into bed—after three movies, a bag of chips, and enough hot chocolate to have her up visiting the bathroom every hour to pee—she'd resigned herself to the fact Leif wasn't coming back.

And while she might be a modern woman, she wasn't the type to start texting someone who'd not given her permission, even if Mindy had the number dropped off with a box of cream puffs.

However, in her diary that night, she did pen a letter to someone she'd not talked to in a while.

Dear Santa...

CHAPTER
ELEVEN

THE OPEN FIRE DIDN'T HAVE ANY CHESTNUTS OR MARSHMALLOWS ROASTING...

Santa's mansion smoldered for most of the next day—blame the thick logs that were used in its construction. Despite the intense heat, nothing else around the abandoned home had burned. The elves and other inhabitants had formed a bucket brigade that saved all the other buildings. It seemed the best course of action once they realized no amount of water would stop the inferno that took the once-grand home.

A sobering loss. Apart from the massive trunks used to shape the walls, it also had stone for the giant hearth. The windows had held stained glass pieces of art. Inside, it had offered comfort via big couches and overstuffed chairs, fur rugs not yet replaced by the kinder synthetic type. Santa's home had been abandoned in a time when such things were considered acceptable. It had been vacant since his imprisonment. His wife, rather than remain living there, disappeared.

No one had the heart to touch it, as if they all secretly

hoped that one day the big man would return to his senses, somehow beat back the evil inside, and return to the village. Leif doubted it. Whatever escaped that pit likely wouldn't be in the mood to make toys and spread joy.

But that monster might have wanted to send a warning. Was Krampus to blame for the house burning down? If yes, how had he or one of his agents entered the secure village?

Did it matter? The end result proved to be the same. A somber Leif stood vigil with the others through the night, watching as a legacy burned to the ground. Some cried at the sight, his mother included. She stood on one side of Leif, head on his arm. His father pretended to not be wiping his eyes when turned away.

Once the wood turned to ash, the mourning ended. The mansion was gone. Christmas approached. Time to get to work.

The elves snapped to attention and moved from the ruin, Leif splitting off from them as they headed for the factories and other jobs in the village. For him, the next step involved a few hours' sleep at his apartment to clear his head then back Bella's to look for clues to find Krampus, of course.

The buckle on his belt buzzed. He really wanted to ignore it. Fatigue taffy-fied his limbs and thoughts.

Bzzzt.

An elf never shirked his duty. He clicked. "Blitzen."

"Your father wants a report."

The same father who stood right beside him during

the mourning period. But rather than hang back and ask Leif what he'd seen, he kept things official.

"On my way." He held in a sigh. Leif's steps veered, heading for Jingle Barn, a veritable hive of activity. They'd pulled in some of the older retired elves and reindeer to help. Not that it made a difference. Krampus had escaped the pit and vanished by all appearances. Perhaps with some rest, Leif would figure out what he'd missed.

Entering his father's office, he noticed immediately his mother leaning against the desk. Along with her synthetic leather pants and her vest over the cream turtleneck, she wore that look. The one that brought Leif back to his time as a little elf, still learning and at times being a bit naughty with friends. Painting the penguins as clowns. Getting greased and naked to slide down Peppermint Peak.

The look that said he was about to get in trouble. At his age, ridiculous, but explain that to his mother.

He focused on his father first. "Sir." Officially called to report meant adopting the formal address.

Once his father nodded, Leif then turned to his mother and dipped his chin as he said, "Hello, ma'am." Not Mother until he knew the situation. She also outranked him despite having retired from active reindeer duty.

"Now he has time to say hello, but did he when he popped by last night?" Mother crossed her arms and glared.

Uh-oh. "I was busy."

"Busy taking a stranger to dinner instead of taking a

teensy tiny moment to say hello to his loving mother who pushed out his gigantic head after twenty-seven hours of labor."

Moments like these he wished he could lie. He even knew what he'd say, *I didn't want to wake you*. Instead, he argued with her the only way he knew how, the way she taught him. "I tried calling you earlier that day, but you didn't answer. Guess you had more important things to do than talk to your only son."

Rather than justify or counter his rebuttal, his mother beamed. "Clever boy."

"Not really," his father grumbled. "A clever boy would have found the target."

"I'm working on it. It hasn't been easy given Krampus has managed to lie low and not draw attention." Leif liked failing about as much as his father did, which was to say not at all.

"Subtle is not how Krampus operates. We should have seen casualties by now." His father shoved out of his chair and pointed to a screen with moving boxes of data. News from around the world. Reports. Anything they could find.

Leif had a possibility. "What if he didn't escape? Maybe whatever took down that mountain actually managed to kill him."

"It would be foolish to believe that."

"Has anyone gone down to look?"

His father's expression said it all. "Krampus is alive and out there. I'm sure of it. Which is why I don't understand your actions. Who was that woman? Why did you bring a human here? We are under high alert." His father tucked his hands behind his back as he barked at him.

"The alert is to watch for the enemy. Bella is not the enemy. I needed her help with something."

"Does that help have anything to do with the fact you missed a button dressing?" His mom's gaze dropped for a second to his jeans where he'd skipped a loop.

Foiled because he'd chosen to not wear zippers after getting his tender bits caught one too many times. His cheeks heated. "Bella was attacked by gingerbread," he blurted out in an attempt to save himself.

"Are you telling me that woman couldn't handle one cookie?" Said with some disdain by his mom.

"Actually, she crushed eight dozen. But then they fused together into a giant cookie."

"Impossible," Father blurted out.

Mother blanched as she said, "Can you explain?"

"I didn't see the initial smushing and joining together, but according to Bella, she found a bunch of living cookies in her store. They attacked her with knives and forks."

"Gingerbread aren't violent. Mischievous, yes. Even sly and tricky. But they don't harm people." His mother had shifted from the desk to move closer to his father, who placed an arm around her.

"She has the marks on her ankles to prove it."

"You said the remains fused and returned to life?" his father questioned softly.

"After Bella crushed them, she left to get a dustpan. Gone a few minutes only. When she returned to her shop, the cookies had disappeared, every single crumb. That was when the giant version attacked and tossed her through the window of her shop. Reiver and I arrived as she was fighting it off."

"And took care of it." His father scribbled on a sheet in front of him. A tablet actually that took the information electronically, but it acted as a traditional notepad for his father, who hated technology. A dying breed of elf.

Leif couldn't wait until they upgraded their communications devices. Talking to his groin because they wouldn't shift away from the buckle earned him plenty of odd looks when among people outside the village.

"Actually, it wasn't me who ended it. Although I tried. Reiver and I both slashed and hacked, but it just kept reattaching its limbs. I took off its head three times, and it kept getting back up."

"Wait, you decapitated it and it didn't die?" his mother queried.

He nodded.

His father paused to eye him over his small, round glasses. "This inability to kill it... Does this mean there is a giant, violent cookie rampaging somewhere?"

"No, because Reiver's wife is friends with some goblins, who ate it."

His father blinked before scribbling the details.

"Did those goblins show signs of wanting to join together after?" His mother's morbid question.

"Not that I know of." It never occurred to him to even check.

"How odd you happened to be in the right place at the right time," his father mused aloud.

"Not really that odd. Given my lack of progress on the case, I went to see Daphne. She suggested I visit Reiver."

"And yet, Reiver isn't who you brought to dinner." A less-than-subtle nudge for information by his mother. She wouldn't give up until he spilled the jellybeans.

Leif gave in with a sigh. "Her name is Bella. She owns the Christmas shop that was attacked."

His father cleared his throat. "Let me get this straight. You rescued a stranger being attacked by unnatural cookies and immediately thought it a good idea to bring her to our hidden village."

He winced at his father's summary. "You have nothing to worry about."

"Don't we, though?" his father harangued. "Every year, through accident and loose lips, more and more humans are learning about us."

"And?" Leif was of the new generation that thought it might be time to stop living in secret.

"And it's only a matter of time before the wrong sort try to infiltrate and steal from us."

"Will they? Steal what? What do we do that they can't?" he pointed out. "Humans these days have their own factories to build anything they want."

"It's not just the toys we worry about. What if they try and steal our portal magic?" Father argued.

"And so what if they do? Can you imagine a world that wouldn't have to rely on polluting trucks and ships to transfer goods? And besides, they wouldn't be using them for long once people started disappearing." They'd learned over the years that while inanimate objects never had issue, not so for living things. Use it too often and sometimes travelers didn't exit on the other side. Most assumed the voice that lived within the null world of the portal got them. This danger was why portal use was heavily restricted among the elves and other living beings.

Mother snapped her fingers. "Why don't we worry about portals and human and elf race relations after we've dealt with the Krampus situation. Most especially why you believe a woman selling holiday trinkets is involved."

"I don't know if she is, but I do find it curious that the gingerbread wanted something from her."

"What?" his father barked.

Leif had to shrug. "No idea."

"Is it possible it got away with what it sought?" his mother asked.

"Not unless we missed a cookie."

"What does this have to do with you bringing her here?" his father demanded.

"When I searched her shop and apartment, I didn't find anything that made me tingle. But she had this box from her mother, and she wouldn't let me see inside."

"Didn't you tell it was a matter of Christmas Emergency?"

"I did, but she didn't believe me. Hence why I brought her here. I wanted to prove I truly was one of the elves from Santa's Village."

"You should have shown her your ears," his father grumbled.

"She saw them and didn't think it proved anything because anyone can get those nowadays with plastic surgery."

"Ridiculous," his mother huffed. "Treating an elves unique nature as if it were a fashion accessory."

Leif once more rolled his shoulders. "I don't understand why people do it, but it happens. Anyhow, Bella wanted irrefutable proof that I was who I claimed to be."

"If she didn't believe the elf part, why didn't you flip into your reindeer shape and fly around her living room?" Again, his father just had to throw common sense at him.

"Uh." Leif had no reply because that would have been the easier solution.

His mother saved him. "What our son means to say is he had only a moment to come up with a plan, and so he chose to bring her to the village, show her why she should help, and took her to dinner to... You know, I'm not quite sure I understand why you took her to dinner at your favorite restaurant."

Well played. Not quite a question but it required a truthful answer. "I wanted to delay her departure because I enjoy her company," he admitted, and his mother clapped her hands, huffing, "Aha!"

He wasn't sure if that was a good or bad exclamation. He definitely didn't want to deal with it right now.

Rather than hammer him, his mother approached

and bussed his cheek. "I'm making turkey pot pie and a baguette for dinner. Bring the woman."

The invitation froze Leif into place. Not because his mother expected to meet Bella but because she assumed Leif would see her again. He was, but he didn't like she'd guessed it. "I doubt I'll be back that soon."

"Very well. When you return."

Mother left, and Leif sighed even louder than before. "I'm so screwed."

"In her defense, she's been waiting a long time for you to find your special gift."

"Bella is a person, not a present."

"You going to tell me she's not the thing you've wanted all your life?" Father arched a brow.

"We just met a day ago." A feeble argument that his father countered with something Leif already knew.

"The moment I met your mother I knew she'd be my wife."

"That was you and Mom. I barely know Bella."

"I'm sure you'll rectify that. When are you seeing her again?" Not would, but when.

Again, he couldn't lie. "Soon."

"I'm surprised you're delaying your return."

"What's that supposed to mean?"

"Think of it, gingerbread that don't die easily? That's some powerful magic. I wonder who cast the spell."

The reminder had Leif frowning. "Whoever did it might still be around." He rubbed his face. "Shouldn't the real question be, is this tied to Krampus?"

"What you described is a perversion of Christmas magic. What do you think?"

"Sounds like it could be Krampus." It would explain why Daphne recommended he visit Reiver.

"I think you should return to this Bella's side as soon as possible. After all, we don't know if the magic user will make another attempt."

"I'll return immediately, sir." His elation helped with the fatigue.

"Not that quick. Grab a few hours' sleep first. Oh, and a bath. You're a little rough."

"What if another cookie or worse confronts Bella?"

"Isn't that hunter you went to school with nearby?" His father rubbed his chin.

"Right across the road."

"Good. I'll contact him and ask if he can watch over her until you arrive. With Christmas only days away, we can't take any chances. If she has something Krampus wants, then we need to find it first."

An ominous note to exit on. Hopefully Reiver answered Leif's father and agreed. Otherwise, his father might send someone else. Like Joel Prancer. He had all the ladies, and some of the men, swooning over him. Then again, that would be the least of his worries. Mother appeared way too interested in the Bella situation. More than likely, at this very moment, she plotted matchmaking mayhem to try and get him married. She took it as a personal affront her only son had yet to get hitched. All of the other reindeer were laughing and calling her names.

But Leif wouldn't get married just to please his mother. He'd marry for love.

A thought accompanied by Bella's face.

Could it be?

It happened that quick for his parents. Even if he believed it possible, what about Bella? What if she didn't feel the same?

Only one way to find out. He had to return and see where things would go. Right after that nap and shower because he smelled worse than a cranberry brie dropped on top of a burning Yule log.

He made it almost all the way home before a petite elf, wringing her braid between her hands, waylaid him. She wore the white camouflage of a soldier who worked outside the village. They had troops scattered in the North and even South Poles providing surveillance and protection.

"Excuse me, Blitzen, sir." She yanked her twisted hair in anxiousness.

"Afternoon, soldier. How can I help you?" He paused to give her his attention. It seemed to render her more nervous, and her gaze went all around, not once focusing on him.

"I am really, really sorry to bother you, but I know something about..." She glanced around before lowering her voice to whisper, "*His* escape."

That drew his attention, as did her furtive nature. "What do you know?"

"Can we go somewhere private?" she asked, so low he barely heard her.

"My place is just upstairs." When she appeared unsure, he added, "I've got cocoa."

"Add a shot of something to warm the belly and you're on."

"I've got just the thing. Shall we?" He inclined his head toward the building in front of them, a dark-blue-painted wood trimmed in resin of varying cyan hues. Walking in brought them into an atrium where the sun shone through the clear window that spanned the height of the building. It kept the space warm enough to grow some grass, flowers, and even an apple tree.

Ringing the courtyard were balconies linked by stairs for the apartments. Leif had the top floor. He took the steps easily, and the petite elf, firmly gripping her braid, followed him, jumping when he shut the door of his apartment behind them.

To put her at ease, he moved into his kitchen and prepared the drink, asking casually, "What's your name?"

"Sonya, sir."

"Call me Leif. Now tell me why you sought me out, Sonya."

"Because you're looking for *him*."

"I am. What do you know about the prisoner's escape?"

"I am—was—one of the guards in the South."

"Were you working the day he got out?" Leif treaded softly, mostly because he'd read the reports. All the guards in the South had been questioned about that day and asked about their prisoner. None of them had anything to say.

At all. Peculiar, and more signs that Krampus got help.

"I was supposed to be on shift when it happened, only I got sick and my cousin Paisleigh took my place. Because of me, she almost died." Sonya's lip trembled.

"Is she the one they pulled out of the glacier's rubble?" Out of the four guards on shift, only one had been recovered.

Sonya nodded. "Paisleigh is the only one who escaped that day."

"We talked to your cousin. She doesn't know what happened." She remembered nothing of her last shift, not even why she'd obviously been in the tunnel when the glacier collapsed.

"Paisleigh wasn't involved. She had no idea." The braid yanking grew harder as the elf's agitation increased.

"No idea about what?" he prodded gently.

"We didn't see the harm." Sonya paced his living room.

"Harm in what?"

"She just wanted to talk to him. She looked so sad."

"Who?" His patience reached the end of his popcorn-threaded rope.

"Mrs. Claus." Sonya turned to face him "She came to the glacier a few weeks ago when I was on duty. Asked for some time alone to talk to her husband. We didn't see the harm."

"We?"

"Me, Maurice, Helga, and Bjorn."

"Those last three are the names of the missing guards from the night he escaped." Thought to be dead, but now he had to wonder.

"You think I don't know that?" she groaned.

"Tell me about Mrs. Claus."

"She looked the same as her picture, but sad."

"You're sure it was her?"

"Oh yes, there was no doubt. But what she asked…" Sonya stopped pacing to stare out his window. "We knew our job. It's not like we just said yes right away when she asked to see him. We discussed it first."

He guided her gently. "Who did you discuss it with?"

"Just the four of us. Which I know was wrong." She hung her head. "It was the middle of the night, and she pleaded with us to not tell anyone."

Given who did the begging, he could see why they had strayed from their mission.

At the same time, optimism tried to unfurl within. Was this the clue they'd been seeking? "You're saying you allowed Mrs. Claus to go under the glacier?"

She nodded.

"Did you leave her alone at any time?" He suspected he knew the answer.

Sonya confirmed. "Not for long and she didn't bring anything with her when she went in, nor carry anything when she came out."

"You obviously searched her before letting her in?"

"No." A low whisper. "It was Mrs. Claus."

A woman missing for decades. Someone dearly loved by the elves. He could see why they'd given her a free pass, even as he suspected they finally had the answer as to who helped Krampus escape.

"How long was she inside?"

"Not long. Ten minutes, maybe fifteen."

"Where did she go when she left?"

"I don't know. None of us remember seeing her go. And Helga didn't even recall her visiting in the first place. It's like a hazy dream."

More memory tricks. "The room, did you inspect it after she left?"

"Yes, but there was nothing to see. The grate and magic remained intact. We didn't hear or see a thing. Nothing happened at all until weeks later when it all collapsed."

He rubbed his face. "Who else have you told?"

"No one. Once I realized Helga didn't remember, I was afraid."

"You should be because the error you made wasn't in letting Mrs. Claus visit but waiting so long to tell us." Knowing she was involved gave them another avenue of search.

Wrong answer, as Sonya's eyes sparked with agitation. "This is why I didn't want to say anything. Mrs. Claus is good. She would never hurt us."

"No, but her husband would."

CHAPTER
TWELVE

WEARING A SWEATER WITH TWO STRATEGICALLY PLACED BOWS...

THE NEXT CUSTOMER TO THE SHOP FOUND BELLA UNDER THE tree, in plaid slacks, with her butt in the air.

At the jingle of the bell, she shouted, "I'll be with you in a second." She just wanted to finish positioning the skirt.

"Don't hurry on my account. I'm enjoying the view."

Leif! Her head lifted too fast, hit a branch, her hair got caught, the whole tree swayed, and Bella froze as Leif chuckled.

"Hold still. I'll help you get loose."

Deft fingers, gentle and quick, helped her untangle without damage. She gasped when she slid out from under the tree and found herself hoisted to her feet, facing a smiling elf with a twinkle in his eye.

Her heart skipped a beat. He'd returned. What did it mean?

"Hi," she managed to mutter.

"Hello to you, too. Sorry it took me so long to return."

"Guess you were busy."

"Too busy," he grumbled. "I meant to return earlier. I'm very glad to see you." His lips pressed to hers in a light kiss of hello.

She flung her arms around him and embraced him back firmly and with tongue. They eventually broke apart, rather breathless.

He chuckled. "Well, that is a nice hello."

"I'm glad to see you." Her shy admission.

"As if I could stay away." He stroked a finger down her cheek.

"Is everything okay in the North Pole?"

He grimaced. "Yes and no. We had a fire."

"Oh no!"

"Luckily only one building was lost and no one hurt."

"Was it an accident?" She'd stopped using candles when she got Big Fluff. One hairy tail almost igniting was enough to convince her to try rechargeable solar-powered versions instead.

"They need to wait for it to cool to find out how it started. And then, before I could even hit a shower, some new information arose in the Krampus investigation that required looking into."

"Oh? What did you find out?"

"His wife appears to be the one who helped him escape."

"Mrs. Claus?" She huffed on a high note. "Oh, that's sweet."

A brow angled in sync with his confused, "Sweet how?"

"Because even after all this time, she must love him if she wanted to set him free."

"The thing in that prison isn't her husband anymore. Her actions have put everyone in danger." Leif rubbed a hand over his face.

"Has anyone talked to her?"

"Can't because she's disappeared. No one knows where's she's gone or how to find her."

"I'm sure you'll catch a break soon."

"Maybe." He didn't sound so certain. "What about you? Any problems with cookies or other things while I was gone?"

She shook her head. "Not a thing."

He glanced past her. "I see you got the window fixed. Sorry I wasn't here to help."

"Mindy knew someone, thankfully. My biggest problem was my mom. When she found out about the vandalism, she wanted me to go stay in a hotel." She rolled her eyes.

"She has a point. Staying elsewhere would have made you safer in case that person animating cookies returned."

"If I'd left, how would you have found me?"

"I can't tell you. North Pole secret." He winked.

The teasing brought a smile to her lips. "I'm glad you came back."

He reached for her hand, squeezing it as he murmured, "Me, too."

The intimate moment was shattered as a customer entered, followed by another. Leif slipped into the role of salesclerk easily and oddly. Odd because it felt comfortable. She glanced at him often, and when he caught her, he would offer her a wink or a grin.

When they got a break, she had to ask. "Shouldn't you be looking for Krampus?"

"Who says I'm not? Right now, you and your shop are my only lead. Maybe being here will give me a clue."

"And if it doesn't?"

"Then perhaps tonight we should explore the town."

"We?"

"I thought you might want to join me."

"Are you asking me to help you hunt down a murdering Christmas monster?" Not how she would have pictured her evening.

"Yes and no. We're not looking to apprehend or contain, merely locate. Once we have a position, I can call in the squads to handle Krampus."

"So we're just going to wander around hoping to come across a clue?"

"It's not a great plan, I admit. However, as someone reminded me, the spell on those gingerbread had to be cast by someone."

"You think they're still around?"

"Perhaps they didn't go far and are waiting for a second chance."

"Unless they're portal hopping like you."

"Portal magic isn't that readily accessible."

"Meaning what exactly?"

"For one, not just anyone can create a portal. It takes a certain kind of specialized magic. There is an entire team of elven mages who work in rotation to ensure the functioning of the village square portal."

"So only elves can create them?"

"I believe there are some groups of people who can also open portals, like humans for example, but it's a rare ability. I can't create one. It's why I have to rely on this." He indicated his decorated tree buckle.

"Should we be looking for an elf? After all, you did say bringing gingerbread to life was a North Pole kind of thing."

His lips twisted. "Yes, living gingerbread are the occasional byproduct of elf baking. One at a time. I've never known anyone to do it intentionally and in great number. Not to mention, the giant living cookie we fought... I've never seen or heard of anything like it."

"It's got to be because of Krampus," Bella stated.

"Maybe. Although I don't think he was directly involved in the cookie attack. More like his will being done."

"Wait, Krampus has minions?" For some reason this blew her mind. "Who would want to serve him?"

"How does any evil leader find followers?"

"That is disturbing on so many levels," she observed.

"Agreed, but it might be the break we need. If we can track down the person who animated those cookies, they might be able to lead us to Krampus or his lair."

"Okay, but how are we supposed to find that person? Because I highly doubt us walking the streets will result in running into them. How would we even know who it was? They wore a cloak, and I'm pretty sure they don't have a tattoo that screams 'Evil Minion.'"

"That would be the hole in my plan," he admitted. "But I've been racking my brain, and I am out of ideas."

"There has to be way to draw them out." She chewed the tip of her thumb. "Whoever it was thought I had something."

"Yes. But given they didn't bother you yesterday, or even today, it appears they might have changed their minds."

"Or I don't have what they want. Yet."

"What do you mean yet? I thought you weren't expecting any packages."

"I'm not. You know that and I know that, but does whoever was looking know that?"

He blinked. "I am not sure I followed that."

"Those cookies came very specifically to my shop and left empty-handed."

"Actually, they didn't leave, they were digested."

She grimaced. "Don't remind me. Anyhow, they didn't get what they wanted, so whoever sent them is either thinking A"—she ticked a finger—"when can I try again? B, who actually has whatever it is I want, or C"—she held up a third finger—"what if it hasn't arrived yet?"

"Not sure how that helps us."

"What if we made the cookie animator believe it was C. Not yet received. If we could somehow convince them I got a package with what they want, then we might lure them out of hiding and catch them in a trap."

A plan suddenly unfolded in her head. The problem was in convincing Leif to let her be the bait.

He got his jolly self into a snit when she insisted on helping. "I am not putting you in danger."

"It's my choice," she argued.

Rather than fight with him about it, she pulled out some fruitcake and syrup. A syrup she didn't so accidentally spill in his lap.

Once she'd licked him clean of the sticky stuff, he gasped, "You win. We'll try your idea."

CHAPTER
THIRTEEN
OH, HOLY NIGHT, HIS IRE WAS BRIGHTLY SHINING...

One good climax deserved another. Leif didn't leave Bella hanging after the BJ was over. He made sure she got equal orgasmic treatment. And then, while she was still glowing from it, he reneged.

"Forget what I said before. I am not comfortable using you as bait." Putting her in danger didn't feel right.

"You don't really have a choice. Who else can pull it off? I'm the only employee here. Besides, it's a good plan."

It was. And at the same time, he didn't lie when he said. "No, it's not because it puts you in danger."

"I would rather be the hunter than the hunted," she stated. "I'm less likely to be surprised."

He pressed his lips tight but couldn't deny her logic. "Very well. We'll try it."

"Awesome. Which reminds me, you should probably keep a low profile because if they're watching they might not fall for our trick if they realize who you are."

"Or we could make them think you hired someone and I become the bait."

"I'm a strong independent woman. I don't need you protecting me," she hotly retorted.

"I know," he admitted on a sigh. His mother would smack him for trying to be overprotective. Especially since he wasn't being rational. Bella actually had a sound idea for drawing out anyone possibly watching her shop. She suggested going to the post office, only a few blocks on foot, and exiting with a package or two. If someone watched, perhaps they'd be tempted to invade her shop again.

And try they would. According to Mindy, three massive and separate orders for gingerbread cookies had been picked up at bakeries around town. Those same bakeries, when questioned, couldn't provide a description of the client. Reiver had been the one to visit them all and then report to Leif about his failed endeavor. None of the bakeries could offer a description of the bulk cookie buyer because they came in wearing a voluminous coat that went down to the calves, with a hood, sunglasses, and an N95 mask, claiming a compromised immune system. They paid cash.

The orders totaled three hundred and forty-four gingerbread people. The spell caster had bought enough to form a cookie army.

Not good. Would those animated baked treats come after Bella again? They certainly might if she went through with the plan. At the same time, what choice did they have? Christmas was days away. They had to do something.

Which was why he agreed, but with some modifications to her idea.

They hashed out the finer points upstairs in her apartment over delivery pizza, along with Mindy and Reiver, who brought a decadent frothy mint mousse chocolate dessert served with hot cider.

Everyone was on board, so why did he feel like he'd eaten too many sweets?

When Reiver and Mindy left, he sat on the couch beside Bella, their sides touching but nothing else because Big Fluff chose to inhabit his lap and demanded petting. Whenever he stopped, the feline dug in her claws. While fear was part of the reason he stroked, he actually did enjoy the soft fur and the rumble of contentment.

"Big Fluff likes you," Bella observed, looking relaxed and beautiful leaning against him.

"You sound surprised."

"She barely likes me," she admitted, peeking at him with a grin.

His lips quirked. "I find that hard to believe."

She blushed and glanced away. "So, you're okay with the plan?"

Not really. Rather than lie, he said, "When I leave here to plant the packages at the post office, I want you to lock all the doors."

"I will."

"Don't let anyone in."

"Not even you?" she teased.

"This isn't funny. We need to be careful. It's only days until Christmas, meaning Krampus is at his most dangerous."

"To bad children. I'm hardly a child." Her nose wrinkled.

"There's something different about him this time. He's not acting like he should." Still no bodies piling up anywhere.

"Maybe he learned his lesson."

"And if he didn't? Not a chance we can take."

"What time are you taking the decoys over?"

"Not until the streets are quiet."

"Wouldn't it be easier to portal inside?"

"It would, but I've done too much traveling that way recently."

"Is using a portal bad for you? Are they like radioactive or something?" Her eyes widened as she gazed on him with concern.

"Not radioactive, but they can become dangerous to individuals if used too often too quickly. Besides, in this situation, since I don't know what kind of security I'd be landing in, it's best I go carefully. I might have to disable some video cameras."

"Will that take long?"

"Depends on the setup."

"If you're waiting for the street to quiet, then we've got at least an hour or two to wait. Whatever will we do?" A coy thing to say that had him chuckling.

"I know what I'm thinking."

"Would it have something to do with paying me back for the syrup I spilled earlier?"

"Maybe," he teased.

"Forget maybe." She turned to face him fully, and their lips met in a clash.

CHAPTER
FOURTEEN
GLAD SHE'D WORN MATCHING RED POINSETTIA-PRINTED SATIN UNDIES AND BRA...

Bella had never wanted anyone more than Leif. How else to explain why she'd shamelessly poured syrup all over his groin, and then, rather than let him go shower, she'd flipped the sign to Closed and sucked him clean.

But the back room of the shop wasn't the place to have sex. Here and now, though, in her apartment, just the two of them... She dumped Big Fluff into the living room and closed the bedroom door. She went after his clothes, practically ripping them from his body.

Leif's hands proved just as busy, stripping her before dragging her naked body close for a kiss. Their lips meshed, and she melted in his arms, flesh to flesh, every part of her tingling.

When her legs sagged, her knees refusing to work, he laid her upon the bed, and she stared at him, eyes hooded with arousal. She licked her lips at the sight of his erect manhood. Long and thick, she couldn't wait to feel it inside her.

But he made her wait.

Leif teased, running a finger down her body, starting from the valley between her breasts, over her rounded tummy, through the curls of her mound to the vee of her thighs. She parted them in invitation, and he growled.

"Don't rush me."

"Maybe I want you to rush." She reached for him.

"I'm going to take my time and enjoy this moment if you don't mind."

"Fine. If you insist," she said with an exaggerated sigh.

"Naughty so close to Christmas?"

"Very naughty," she purred as he leaned down enough that she could drag him close for a kiss. His body covered hers, hard and lean, the throb of his erection trapped between their bodies. She shifted her thighs, hoping he'd get the hint.

Instead, he broke the kiss and murmured, "Slow."

She didn't want slow.

She didn't have a choice.

He nibbled the edge of her jaw then the column of her throat. He pressed his mouth to the pulse on the side of her neck. From there, he slid his mouth down to her breast, where he circled around her nipple. Teasing. He used his tongue to trace all around, ignoring how her buds tightened and begged for his attention.

When he finally took the bud into his mouth, she arched and cried out. Grabbed his head. Encouraged him to suck. Which he did, slowly…

And just as her toes curled, he switched sides and started over.

Soon she panted and writhed, wet between her legs, aching and wanting. He kissed his way down her body, circling her navel with his tongue before continuing his journey south.

He nuzzled her mound, and she shivered. He slid between her legs, his wide shoulders pushing at her thighs. Teased her by rubbing his jaw and lips against her flesh, ignoring the part that throbbed but for one hot exhalation as he switched legs.

He put his mouth on her just when she thought she might scream. She did cry out and writhed as he licked and stroked her. His tongue worked her sweet spot. His fingers thrust into her and pressed in a place that had her gasping for air.

She was going to come, and she managed to exhale, "I want you inside me."

Instead, he made her climax, thrusting her over an edge that had her thrashing and panting then writhing as he kept licking and finger thrusting, taking her pulsing orgasm and shoving it to another edge.

Only then did he finally shift to position his cock at the entrance of her sex. The tip of him parted her nether lips, and her lips parted in pleasure as he slid into her, stretching her, filling her.

As he began to move, he leaned in and kissed her, a long, intimate meshing of their mouths as he rocked and ground into her in a slow, steady rhythm that gathered speed. Thrusting and grinding. Deep. Hard.

Perfect...

Before she climaxed again, she opened her eyes to find him already watching her. Their gazes locked, heightening the intensity.

They came together, a rolling, rollicking orgasm that would have had her shouting Hallelujah if she had any breath.

He collapsed beside her and tucked her close against him. They said nothing. Why bother when the moment was already so perfect?

She could have stayed cuddled all night, but Leif rose just after midnight. Time to put their plan into play.

He covered her with a blanket, whispering, "I'll be back as soon as I can. Sleep easy. Reiver's watching outside."

She heard the slide of a window then a metallic clang as he landed on the fire escape bolted to the side of the building above the alley. The draft ceased as the window shut, and a happy, tired Bella fell asleep, thinking of her lover and—

She startled awake and lay in her bed, holding her breath. Something woke her. Probably Leif returning. She rolled over to greet him, sure he'd just come in by the window. After all, there was a definite cool draft. Her lips parted to say his name, only to pause as she realized Leif hadn't returned. The window remained closed. Could be he'd come in and gone into the living area.

She didn't believe that for one second. The hairs on her body stood like good little nutcracker soldiers, stiff at attention. Her next exhalation steamed in the cold air.

Uh-oh. Not good and she was naked in bed! Definitely a situation requiring action. Starting with underwear.

Quietly. She didn't want to draw attention. Maybe she was scared over nothing. Wouldn't be the first time she'd freaked herself out, but this was the first time every single breath she made frosted in her home. A home kept at a solid seventy degrees.

Tell that to the white mist that hung in the air.

While not a slob, Bella did have some lazy habits that came in handy. Since she was a clean underwear kind of girl, she had one drawer dedicated to her undies, and it usually hung partially open so she could just snag a pair easily.

It meant she could flip a pair over her naked pie in quick order. Then, because she was so freaking cold, she snared the Oodie hanging over the chair kept in the corner, whose sole purpose in life was to hold the clothes that weren't dirty enough for the wash but worn enough to not go back in the closet as clean. The Oodie covered her upper body and arms but left most of her legs bare.

Still no noise from the other room. She was acting crazy. Woke and imagined—

Huff. The white fog mocked her attempt to rationalize because she couldn't explain it. She did know to fear it, though. Had something worse than gingerbread come to visit? She could either hide or find out.

What if there was nothing there and she hid? How foolish would she feel?

Then again, what if she wasn't alone?

Then she'd fight with—

She glanced around her bedroom and saw nothing meant for murderous or protective intent. Perhaps she should look at getting a sword or, at the very least, a long knife to hang on the wall in her room. Not a gun, though, they scared her.

She ended up grabbing her tablet, hard surface and swingable. If she could get to the front hall, she had an umbrella hung on the hooks by the door. It would make a good whacking weapon.

If someone was there.

Could be she heard her cat, although that would be a first. Big Fluff always slept with her at night. Not in her bed, but in the room.

Somewhere.

A quick glance at the usual spots didn't net her fluffy feline. She might have chosen to lounge under the bed. Wouldn't be the first time. Nothing like a paw suddenly swiping at an ankle to get a person moving quick in the morning.

Bella had almost reached the door when fabric rustled from the living room. One foot in the air, she paused.

Someone was there!

She took a breath. Calm. Rational. Probably just Leif making himself a snack, trying to not wake her up.

But what if it wasn't him?

She cautiously slid into her main living area, the lights of her tree giving everything a soft glow.

No Leif. No one at all. She stepped into the middle of

the room and glanced around at the wall with her television and the fireplace that Mom tried to convince her to remove, claiming they were fire hazards.

As if thinking of Mom were a trigger, her phone rang with that distinctive tune, "Ride of the Valkyries." Why would Mom be calling this late?

She glanced back at the bedroom, where she'd left her cell on her nightstand, charging. Like she always did. Rather than run to grab it, she took another peek around the living room.

Nothing there.

The brush of fur against her leg had her screaming before she could stop herself as Big Fluff bolted past and into the bedroom.

Get a cat, they said. It will be soothing.

Tell that to her racing heart. She'd never go back to sleep now. Might as well wait for Leif. In good news, she no longer saw her breath. It was almost one in the morning, meaning Leif would most likely be returning shortly. A hot cup of milk would be just the thing to put them both to sleep.

As she heated a pot on the stove, she wandered to stand by her window. A gentle snow fell. How pretty.

Explain that to the foreboding in her stomach. Nothing moved outside. Leif had said Reiver would be watching over her while he ran the packages into the post office. Had something happened to him?

Ding.

The faint sound of a bell had her frowning. Had Big

Fluff returned? A pivot had her mentally cataloguing the few bells she had on display.

Ding.

None of them sounded quite like that. She crept carefully from the window, huffing heat into instant mist.

The cold was back.

Ding.

Faint, and yet she'd have sworn it was near. Almost as if it came from—

Ding.

She glanced at her fireplace. It had a cap and mesh to prevent critters at the top. But would it stop Krampus? The very thought only increased her terror.

It wasn't Krampus. He went after bad boys and girls. But Leif said he was acting differently.

Or I'm imagining things? I'm probably still sleeping in my bed, having a nightmare. She thought it and yet retreated a step. Then another, returning to her bedroom, body clammy, breathing hard and foggy. She had to resist the urge to slam the door shut.

A cold draft drew her arms around her upper body. A glance to the window on the alley showed it open, two gingerbread men acting as Atlas, holding it up for the other cookies climbing in.

Run.

The instinct to flee hit, and she opened her bedroom door to a wall of red. Her mouth rounded. She had a moment to recognize who stood in front of her before the sack came over her head.

CHAPTER
FIFTEEN
ALL THAT COULD BE HEARD WAS THE PATTERING OF HOOVES ON THE ROOF...

Leif landed on the slightly angled top of the post office, his hooves kicking up puffs of snow as he slowed his forward momentum. He finished with his racked head held high. It felt good to fly. Since Leif was born after Santa's imprisonment, he never got to do any of Santa's runs. The closest he got was the Kringle Run. A speedy mimic of Santa's route with the best time resulting in first choice for assignments. A coveted thing. He'd not done the Kringle since his twenties. It was something best left to the young.

His good humor almost had him whistling. Bella liked him. A good thing because he liked her a lot. He now wished he'd dumped Sonya's admission about Mrs. Claus and the prison entirely on his dad to deal with. If he'd shirked his duties, reported and ran, he could have been having the best Christmas ever with Bella. However, Leif wasn't the type to walk away without offering to help.

After Sonya told him about Mrs. Claus's involvement, Leif immediately reported to his dad, calling him through the buckle held to his lips, because no way was he talking to his dad via his groin.

The conversation went oddly anyhow.

"I just talked to a Sonya, guard for Krampus, and she says he had a visitor not long before he escaped." He'd paused for effect. *"Mrs. Claus."*

"The guard is certain it was Mrs. Claus?" his father asked.

"Yes."

"Hmm." A less than loquacious reply.

"What's that supposed to mean?"

"Just that it's surprising because she'd already done her yearly visit. Not to mention, she usually never goes to the prison close to Christmas."

An unexpected answer. *"Wait, Mrs. Claus has been visiting Krampus?"* The very idea blew his mind. *"Hold on a second, you knew Mrs. Claus was alive?"*

"When did anyone ever claim she was dead?"

"She left, and, well, I thought..." He'd assumed the fact she'd never resurfaced had meant she'd died until Sonya's story.

"Mrs. Claus suffered tremendous grief when we had to put you know who in the prison. It was a few years before she came for her first visit. Then it became yearly, usually around the summer solstice. She'd give me a ring, and I'd arrange for time for her to visit in private. Which is why I have my doubts as to who Sonya claims to have seen."

"Why would someone fake being Mrs. Claus?"

"Why would someone want to help Krampus escape?"

A good point and reminder. "Would she have helped him?"

"Yes." His father didn't hesitate to reply.

"But obviously didn't in the past, so why now?"

"I don't know."

"Don't you think you should ask her?" Leif drawled. "You know, seeing as you're old friends."

His father cleared his throat. *"I realize this must be a shock."*

"You think?" Leif snapped. "I mean nothing like withholding information."

"She asked for privacy. I gave it."

His father truly didn't see the issue with his actions. Nor did he remember any specifics of the conversation, didn't think it odd he couldn't contact her, and, despite the growing evidence, didn't believe she'd have let Krampus free.

Leif had to wonder if he'd been hexed.

More questioning didn't make the situation any less vague. His father stuck to the basics of his story, and he wasn't alone. Once Leif knew about his father, he began randomly questioning other people. It turned out more than a few people had chatted with Mrs. Claus over the years or done her favors. Like Joobjoob, who made her a large box of her special chocolates for pickup a few times a year. Then there was Klayvis, who'd let her go inside the mansion just the other day.

When Leif asked Klayvis why he'd not told anyone, given the whole fire burning the mansion down, he'd shrugged and said, "No point in wasting your time. Mrs. Claus wouldn't do that."

Funny how her name kept cropping up and no one else's. He especially wondered about the burned house. Accidental or intentional? And if the latter, what had she been trying to hide?

Only ash remained, so he'd never know. Nor did he find out where Mrs. Claus lived when she wasn't picking up chocolate or Mario's caribou sausage or asking his dad to visit Krampus.

Leif's internal magnetic poles were shifting. His straightlaced father had secrets. He had less than a day to find Krampus. He was falling in love with Bella.

Which led to a choice: Chase after the Mrs. Claus angle or trust his gut and stick with Bella?

Standing on the roof of the post office, he didn't regret his choice.

The two front pockets to his coat each held a package, official looking and addressed to Bella, who had the ability to print off shipping labels as part of her thriving online business. Who knew selling Christmas decorations could be so lucrative?

As to how the boxes fit in his coat without causing a bulge? No idea and Leif didn't ask the tailor who'd made his leather duster. That secret design feature belonged to the tailors of the North Pole, who, for some reason, gave the men large-capacity pockets but often left the women grumbling because their garments only had the regular kind, if any at all.

The packages wouldn't be needed until he got inside,

so he left them tucked away for the moment. He just hoped he could figure out how to scan them so that Bella could pick them up in the morning, bait in a plan he still didn't really like. But his only argument—*I don't want to put you in danger*—she'd sunk faster than a melting marshmallow in hot cocoa. This was her choice. He had to respect it.

And he would while watching her the entire time. Unlike a snowman who sometimes braved the sun, hoping he wouldn't melt, he wasn't taking chances. Krampus might mostly work in the dark, but his servants didn't necessarily.

Nothing could happen to her. Not after he'd realized his father was right. He'd just received the one thing he didn't know he needed but now couldn't imagine not having.

Love.

Bella's love.

He might not believe in love at first sight but tell that to how he felt. Fate had jolted him awake, shown him what life could be like, teased him enough he already worried he'd lose it. An elf who lost his other half was a sad elf indeed. Most never recovered and went off never to be seen again. A good thing mated pairs tended to live long and, when they died naturally, were synced to go together. Sad for family and children, but it was the way of the Earth.

Happy thoughts. He shook the sad away. He had a job to do.

Leif located the intake air unit for the HVAC, as most

places had moved away from traditional chimneys. The thought had him freezing. Bella had a fireplace, and he suddenly worried. He'd best hurry because now he couldn't stop thinking about it.

From his inner pocket, he retrieved a metal-legged robotic spider. He held it up and pushed the button on its belly and clearly said, "Unlock the main door." Then he dropped the mechanical tool into the intake tube. The next two he commanded to eliminate cameras.

The North Pole had been on a spree inventing things since the introduction of Eggnog Electronics Factory. The selling of the patents proved lucrative enough to keep their coffers full for the things they couldn't make and had to buy, like bacon and maple syrup.

The launched robots would need time to make their way to their targets; however, patience eluded him this night. Rather than wait for their signal, Leif leaped from roof to the ground, landing lightly, the slight push of his flying magic keeping him from crashing. Broken glass littered the ground in front of the door to the post office.

The frown on his face deepened when he realized it wasn't the work of the robot locksmith. Pulling forth his canes, he approached quietly, wincing as his robot suddenly arrived. With no care in the world, it clicked and whirred, accomplishing the task it was designed for, oblivious to the massive hole already giving Leif entrance.

The door unlocked, noisy and creaky. With the advantage of surprise taken, Leif moved quickly, flowing into the chamber with two of the walls taken up by rectangular mailboxes. No one in here. Probably through the next broken door into the post office itself.

He pursed his lips as he eyed the shards remaining in the frame. He smacked them out of the frame with his rods, wincing at the noise. He'd long lost the element of surprise, but it still bothered him because he might as well put up a flashing sign announcing his arrival.

The next room held posts with chains linking them, creating aisles for clients that led to a long counter. Still no one. He kept his canes at the ready.

Rustling came from beyond the plastic curtain. He didn't hesitate to slide over the counter.

No lights illuminated the back room, a misnomer for the massive space. Towering shelving units stood in a line, sentinels full of packages. Scattered around, large plastic tubs on wheels, the closest one full of letters. A scratched blue one blocked his way down the row facing him, a row that, even with shadows, appeared empty.

Leif treaded softly to the next, ears perked and alert for any whisper of sound. He held his canes down by his sides, empty of magic lest their glow give his position away. The tailors who'd created his coat ensured it made not the slightest bit of noise even when it swayed around his legs.

Sometimes he thought it would be useful to be like Leia Dancer, half reindeer, half wolf, with a nose that could sniff out just about anything. But this close to Christmas, the amount of packages with scented candles clouded his senses. With his sense of smell useless, Leif relied on his gut instinct, which warned him of danger. It would have been more useful to have a direction.

The attack came from above. A glance upwards had him barely lifting his arm in time to block the box falling at him. Despite its size, it didn't weigh enough to actually hurt. Of more concern, the dozen or so gingerbread that dove on him to attack.

"Holy hot cinnamon stick!" Leif savagely swore as he barely batted aside the swipe of a broken piece of glass wielded by a cheerful-looking gingerbread woman. Her skirt was a bright pink to match her lips, her eyeshadow a classic blue.

Her snarl was anything but traditional though, as was her bloodthirsty intent as she hit the floor, bending those cookie knees, and sprang at him.

Leif danced, kicking the cookie and slashing at the same time with his canes, knocking them askew. Twelve cookies might not seem like much. Just like twelve fish the size of a palm seemed benign. Until they ate you because they were piranhas!

A jab in the back of his calf had him yelling, "By Santa's bollocks!" Fierce language from him today as the gingerbread caused damage. But he won. He smashed them to pieces and would have liked a second to enjoy the victory, but someone just had to clock him in the head with a handheld scanner.

"Ow!" He whirled to confront his attacker, only to see more missiles incoming. Packages, rolls of tape in their dispensers, even scissors were being thrown at him. He parried, his canes smacking the danger left and right, falling into a rhythm learned through extensive training. He slapped aside the last thrown package, and silence fell as he stood victorious, a debris field all around him.

A victory short-lived. Leif gaped as the chunks of cookie he'd demolished glowed a most obnoxious green and began pulling together. What in the Christmas cheer was this?!

Mega Cookie hadn't finished forming when Leif chose to remove himself. He didn't have any goblins to eat it, so best not waste time handling it. Not when he could have sworn he spotted movement at the end of the aisle.

"You there. Halt and show yourself. By the authority invested in me by the North Pole Santa Alliance—"

"The Pole can shove a nutcracker where the sun never shines," came the ribald reply.

And all the confirmation Leif needed that someone else was here. He skidded into the junction at the end of the aisle in time to see a figure pause and glance back, its form cloaked not only in fabric but shadow.

"I said halt."

"Halt this." The rude gesture disappeared as the person ran up an aisle.

Leif gave chase, feet digging in as he sought to catch up. He skidded around the corner of the row where he'd seen them disappear.

"Oomph." A harsh exclamation emerged as a wheeled bin slammed into Leif. He shoved it away and jogged to the end, barely pausing as he emerged.

Left or right? He saw no one. Did they hide behind the faint shape of that bin? Just inside a row?

He should have turned on the lights. But then again, he hunted often in the dark because that was the best time to handle monsters.

Since he couldn't trust his eyes, he closed them. His fingers tightened on his canes. Sensitive to magic, they would offer some warning. He listened with his ears, paid attention to his skin. Did it pimple, the hair rise?

He only barely missed being grabbed by the dozen smashed cookies conglomerated together into one of knee height. Moving swiftly, Leif quickly sliced it into pieces. While it regenerated, he loped off, determined to find the animator.

Where could they be?

Back through the front of the store? Or would they try and slip from the back? He'd seen the exit lit in a bright red.

On quiet feet, he sprinted in its direction, hoping he didn't trip over anything. He'd done that once when hunting a blight. A nasty thing recently handled in the wilds of Northern Ontario. No one knew where it came from, but Leif almost went to see his ancestors when he tripped over a rock. Not even a big rock, as Vera taunted him after she'd saved him. But not before she saw Leif gagging when blight drool hit him in the face and some got in his mouth.

Vera also made fun of that.

The reddish glow illuminated the area a little better than other parts. Leif ducked into the shadow before it highlighted him. A stray bin provided covered for his bulk. Only then did he detonate the robots he'd left in the front of the post office.

Bang! Bang! Kapow! Noisy, but doing little damage, the exploding robots only sounded impressive. Would it be enough to flush out the person?

He waited and waited. This time his patience paid off. A scuff of a shoe. The rustle of fabric. A figure, clad head to toe in a voluminous cloak, emerged. An army of cookies at their back.

Uh-oh.

It took them only a second longer to notice his presence. The gingerbread raised up a hue and a cry. "Stranger. Danger."

The person froze then bolted for the door, wobbling oddly.

As cookies went for Leif's ankles, some better armed than others with box cutters, Leif popped to his feet and threw himself at the door.

He tackled the person, his hands tangling in the fabric of the cloak. Thick and slippery at the same time. It might explain why he had a hard time holding on to the person. It didn't help that the wiggling and shoving made no sense. He pinned part of the body and was disturbed when it appeared it split in two.

"What in the mistletoe?" he huffed as the door opened enough for him to see a person about three feet all standing in it.

An elf?

Short like his father, with a bulbous nose and a long

beard, but not one dressed in the cheerful colors of the North, nor in the camouflage of the soldiers, but rather civvies much like Leif.

"Why?" was all he said before someone clocked him from behind.

It loosened his grip on what remained in the cloak, and they shoved Leif off. He hit the floor and rolled, in time to see the gingerbread had returned, bigger than ever.

Not good.

The first elf in the door yelled, "Get moving."

"I'm trying." The second elf struggled to free themselves from the cloak that was partially trapped under Leif, who rolled to avoid a stomping cookie foot. He landed atop the elf, who snarled, "Get off me, dirty caribou."

That was insulting, however not the biggest worry. Leif hauled the elf to his feet then into the air, swinging him to smack the cookie's grasping hand.

"Let me go!" the elf squeaked.

The door began to shut.

Leif ran for it, holding the elf and ramming a shoulder into the closing gap then wedging through. It trapped the gingerbread on the other side. It banged but didn't think to open the door. Not yet at least.

The elf in his grip wiggled, huffing and puffing, using some rude threats that Leif ignored.

The parking lot behind the building held a few cars. Only one of them was driving away.

The elf stopped wiggling and yelled, "You coward. Get back here."

The car didn't slow, and the door to the post office slammed off the wall as the cookie opened it.

"Time to go," Leif announced. He slapped his belt buckle. "I need a portal."

"Again?" huffed Bernie on the other side.

"Yes, again." Leif kept the wiggling elf tucked under one arm while slashing the cookie with the other, taking off an arm then cutting its legs so it fell over.

As he bolted away, Bernie replied, "Give me a second."

"I don't have a second. Giant cookie incoming," Leif yelled as the gingerbread didn't just reassemble; it smiled in his direction.

Bernie huffed. "Sorry. Portal in three, two, one..."

It blazed into existence between Leif and the living cookie.

He dove and emerged in the Village square.

The elf in his grip struggled and cursed. "By the hair on a yeti's butt, let go of me!" But Leif hugged him tight.

What he didn't count on was the giant cookie that came through with him. The gingerbread smack knocked him right off his feet.

Leif fell and dropped his suspect, who scurried to stand behind its creation.

People yelled, and a few panicked and ran away from the monstrous cookie. Leif rose to his feet and sighed at the sight of the giant cookie bearing down on him. Where was a pack of goblins when you needed some?

Then again, did he really need help? They were on his ice. Leif knelt and touched his hand to the cold ground, connecting to the Earth, which surprised some people. As if ice weren't a part of it. Ice was water. Water was life. Life came from Earth.

And what the Earth gave, it could take away.

Magic flowed into Leif, and he rose, his canes glowing, not red and white but the blue-green of the Earth's power. When he sliced the cookie, the burning smell filled the air with acrid spice. One by one, limbs fell to the ground and didn't join back together. He sliced them into pieces, the burning scent of ginger deepening, especially once the magic in the cookie died and the pieces disintegrated.

He left the head for last. The rounded O of its eyes and mouth matched those of its creator. He diced it into little pieces that went poof before turning on his prisoner, who'd wisely not run. Then again, where could he go given the elves surrounding them?

Leif pointed a glowing cane. "As an officer of the North Pole's Santa Authority, I hereby place you under arrest."

"No. I don't have time for this." The elf, obviously lacking proper wits, tried to run.

To where? Leif had no idea. He never even made it out of the square.

It took the citizens only seconds to bind the suspect in Christmas lights and transport him to the Jingle Barn for interrogation.

CHAPTER
SIXTEEN

THE WEE HOURS OF CHRISTMAS EVE AND ABOUT TO START SNOW-JOBBING A PRISONER...

A GRIM LEIF STOOD OUTSIDE THE INTERROGATION ROOM WITH his father. Not his idea. He'd wanted to return to Bella, but when he mentioned it, his father pulled rank.

"You should be here for the questioning. After all, he's your prisoner."

"Bella's alone." His solid argument.

"I thought Reiver was minding her."

"He is."

"And the sorcerer behind the tainted cookies is in our custody."

"He's only half of the duo. The other elf is still out there."

"And probably more interested in hiding now that we're on to them."

Leif couldn't say he shared his father's certainty, but he'd remained because he couldn't deny being curious to the captured elf's motives.

"Have we identified him yet?"

The elf refused to talk. No matter. The Village kept a book of every single birth, marriage, death, exile.

"As a matter of fact, we do know his name. Maurice. Maurice Twinklelights."

The name rang a bell. "Isn't that one of the guards that went missing the night Krampus escaped?"

His father nodded. "We thought him dead, but it appears he might have been part of the plot."

Which boggled Leif's mind. "If he's involved, those other guards working that shift might be as well."

"If that's so, why leave Paisleigh behind?" his father countered.

"Because she wasn't supposed to be there that night. Sonya called in sick."

The reminder had his father frowning. "That would imply a conspiracy."

"And casts doubt on her claim Mrs. Claus visited the prison."

"I'm going to have her brought in for further questioning," his father declared.

Vera, one of the Yule Squad, the fastest of them—courtesy of her Dasher genetics—poked her head out of the interrogation room. "We're ready for you, sir."

His father took a deep breath. He might not like what he'd have to do next, but the safety and security of Christmas had to be preserved.

With a stern expression, Father entered. "So, you're the traitor."

The only thing he said.

The previously uncommunicative prisoner blabbed.

Blame the water he'd been given laced with a minty concoction that loosened the tongue. "Why am I being detained? I did nothing wrong."

"I beg to differ. Let's start with your most recent crime. You broke into a post office," Leif blurted out.

"A *human* post office," Maurice uttered with a sneer. "The Pole has no jurisdiction."

"The creation of animated cookies to commit crimes." Leif threw another accusation.

"Prove it." A smug reply by Maurice.

Father slashed a hand and barked, "Stop with the pile of hot porridge. We know you helped Krampus escape."

"And if I did?" Maurice lifted his chin defiantly.

"Why would you do that?" Once more Leif couldn't contain himself.

Maurice leaned forward, his eyes bright. "The real question is, why were we keeping him locked away?"

Both Leif and his dad ogled the elf before the elder blurted out, "Because he was killing children."

"Bad children," Maurice drawled. "Awful children. The ones that won't ever amount to anything good. Since we locked Krampus away, they've only gotten worse because there are no consequences."

"Murder is a pretty final consequence," Leif pointed out.

"For some, but there are more that will learn a lesson from it."

A hard point to argue; therefore, his father didn't. He went to the heart of the matter. "Where is Krampus?"

A belligerent Maurice crossed his arms and leaned back in this seat. "Don't know."

An elf couldn't lie, but then again, Leif would have sworn an elf wouldn't have seen the release of a child-murdering monster as good.

"You're working for Krampus," Father stated rather than asked.

"So what if I am? We need someone like Krampus in this world if we're going to make a difference before it's too late and the bad overtakes the good."

"You're talking about murder," Leif blurted out.

"Do I need to repeat that children are coming up as naughty in record numbers? They need a firm lesson before it's too late."

"That doesn't mean you release a monster to kill them. Some don't know any better. Others just need more positive influences," Leif argued.

"Some, yes, but most really naughty children will turn into bad adults, and the cycle continues. It has to be nipped in the bud."

Leif felt sick to his stomach. He turned away.

"How did you release Krampus?" his father asked. "Who helped you?"

Maurice shrugged. "Don't know how it was done. As for who helped, you know who was working."

The blatant disregard for his actions had Leif blinking. How could an elf have gone so bad?

A good thing his father knew what to ask because Leif was still stuck on why.

"What were you looking for in that post office?"

Maurice smirked and didn't reply. The potion must have worn off. Would his father give him some more? Unlikely, given it only worked in short bursts and then left the body immune for a few days at least.

They didn't have days.

And Maurice wouldn't talk.

Eventually, his father glanced over his shoulder and gave a nod.

A snowball smacked Maurice in the face.

He blinked, and his expression clearly said they'd have to do better than that.

Leif did his best to not cringe as they tortured the elf. Snow down the back of his shirt. Turkey dinner with all the trimmings, smelling oh so good, out of reach of Maurice. But not Leif and the others, who groaned and smacked their lips as they ate.

But the candy cane that broke Maurice was the pickle-and-jalapeno-flavored one shoved into his mouth. He tried to spit it out but couldn't.

"No. Enough," he gargled around it.

"You ready to talk?" asked Leif's father, who'd remained stern and stoic the entire time.

"Fine. You want to know why I was in that post office? I was looking for Santa's magic," Maurice declared.

The unexpected reply had them pausing a moment before Leif managed to say, "It can be contained in a package?"

"Not all of it. It's why it was split."

"And you thought it might be in that location?"

"Maybe."

Rather than hammer him on that point, Leif shifted. "Why were you looking for a piece of Santa's magic?"

"I'd say the name is kind of self-explanatory." Maurice rolled his eyes.

Leif pressed, "Why do you need it?"

"Well, for one, because it's Santa's magic. And two, we can't exactly let Krampus get a hold of it."

"If you were worried about safety, you should have left Krampus in his prison," Leif's father boomed.

"As if he could be bound forever," Maurice argued.

"Worked just fine for decades," Father snapped.

"We all knew he'd eventually escape. And why not now when the world needs him?"

"The why not is because he's dangerous. What if he doesn't just stick to murdering the bad?"

"We planned for that."

"Planned?" Barely a query, and faintly mocking, but the bragging Maurice didn't need anything more.

"At the time of his release, we had three of the five talismans with Santa's magic. More than enough to keep Krampus in check."

"Why only three? Where was the fourth and fifth?" Leif asked.

"One of them was empty. Someone must have taken the magic before we found it." Maurice complained.

"And the fifth?" Leif reiterated.

His father was the one to murmur, "The idiots gave it to the prisoner."

"Why?"

"So he could escape," Maurice smugly stated.

The elf showed no shame at his actions. "What is wrong with you?" Leif exclaimed.

"We had a plan," Maurice huffed indignantly. "And it would have worked if someone hadn't stolen the three talisman."

"Who stole them?"

Maurice pressed his lips tight.

Before Leif could choose a different tactic, his father spoke. "Who were the talisman stolen from? Not you, obviously. They would have reserved that for the more sophisticated members of your group."

"We're all equal in the NextGen Cabal," Maurice declared.

Leif snapped his fingers. "NextGen Cabal, I've heard of you. You're that movement trying to have Santa removed completely from Christmas and for elves to become its new face." A fad that few ascribed to.

"It's the right thing to do. Elves do all the work!" Maurice huffed.

"Santa is why we are civilized instead of extinct." He'd saved them from slavery to the humans in the old forests of Europe, having discovered their plight during his early Christmas runs.

"We threw off one set of shackles, only to put on a more comfortable pair."

"Radical rabble-rouser," Leif's father huffed. "Shackled my dimpled cinnamon buns. No one in the village has to work. You want to lie abed all day, go ahead. Elves do as they wish and have since the day Santa freed us. But if you want to pretend your life is horrible then go ahead. Just don't drag everyone else down with your belief."

"You're all just penguins following a path blindly until you all run off a cliff."

"That's lemmings, you idiot." Father's dry retort. "And if you're convinced life here is so terrible, then you should have relocated."

"Maybe I will," Maurice snapped.

Given the conversation had devolved, Leif shifted focused away from that topic. "Were you looking for a talisman in that post office?"

"Weren't you?" The sly reply.

"What do the talismans look like? Are they all the same?" Leif kept hammering.

"Hark hear the bells," was the single sung line in reply.

"Bells? How many?" Leif started to ask, only his father interrupted.

"Are you working with Mrs. Claus?"

"No."

"I heard she came by to see him before the escape."

"Bah. She does that time to time." Maurice blew it off.

"Do you know where she is?" Leif asked.

"Nope." Maurice shrugged.

"Where are your accomplices?" Father took the next question.

"As if I'd ever tell."

Frustration pulled at Leif. "Where is your Christmas spirit? We have only one day to stop Krampus."

"And I already told you, I don't want to stop him. In a few years, once the tide has turned, you'll thank the NextGen."

The belief in Maurice just about killed Leif. The elf truly thought he did good.

And in that moment, Leif understood how elves justified doing bad, because he wanted to throttle Maurice, hurt him until he told Leif everything.

Instead, he walked away.

For now.

As an elf, he'd inherited a happy nature, kind and caring and also very forgiving. But he also inherited a reindeer side, where killing happened in the herd if something posed a threat.

Hopefully it wouldn't come to that, but at the same time, Christmas had to be preserved at all costs.

His father joined him a moment later. "He knows more."

"I'm sure he does, but he knows that we know that he knows the longer he holds out, the more likely we can't stop what's about to happen."

"He'll talk." A grim stance by his father.

"We don't have time for you to apply all of the nutcrackers we keep in the village. We need to know where those bells are."

"Obviously not where they're looking," his father's less than helpful response.

It led to him giving his elder a serious look. "Did you know about these bells with Santa's magic?"

His father shrugged. Instead of replying. He avoided lying.

Leif felt himself tensing. Rather than lash out, he chose to get away. "I'm going back to Bella's."

"Is that wise? Maurice didn't seem to think she had the talisman. Why else go looking elsewhere?"

"Maybe we missed something. I don't have any other leads other than Bella, and I've left her alone too long already."

"You're going to portal again?" His father lifted a brow. "Is that wise given how many trips you've made in the last few days?"

He grimaced. "I don't have a choice. The good news is no voices yet. And from here on out, I'll stick to calling for backup."

"Speaking of backup, maybe I should send a few of the squad with you." His father tugged his beard.

More eyes and ears couldn't hurt. The Yule Squad could be stationed on the roofs and street, while he guarded Bella from inside. At least until after Christmas when Krampus was no longer a threat.

"That's a great idea. Send them over once you find them. I'm leaving now." Before his father could start again, Leif left the Jingle Barn at a fast pace to the square.

Out in the human world, being able to portal from any spot proved handy. But Santa's Village blocked portaling from anywhere but the square.

He slapped his buckle the moment he hit the

boundary for it, picturing his coordinates, ignoring the pointed, *"Back there again?"* from Bernie in dispatch.

The swirl he needed appeared, and he didn't hesitate but stepped in. A numbing chill hit, long enough he could think, *This isn't normal*, then a spasm of panic as he wondered if he was lost.

Fear came last with a sibilant whisper. *"Hello, there. Who are you?"*

Leif flailed in nothingness and emerged, breathing hard, in Bella's living room. The unnatural chill pimpling his skin didn't come from the portal, though. The apartment held a limn of frost that shocked him into taking a breath. He choked, not on the cold air but the strange magical residue within it.

Even as he fought against it, a realization hit him hard. Bella. Danger.

A glance around didn't show her in the living room or kitchen. He raced to the bedroom where he'd left her asleep. Beautiful and naked, vulnerable. Unprotected.

The bed appeared disturbed and empty. More frost covered the space, even the cat. Only Big Fluff's eyes showed signs of life. Angry life. Leif placed his hand on the feline, giving some Christmas cheery warmth to counter the cold.

"Meow."

An indignant Big Fluff trotted out to the living room. The space showed no sign of struggle, but the lingering chill and magic made it clear he'd arrived too late. A text to Reiver had a chilling reply.

No one went in or out. Meaning they most likely used a portal or flew.

The door to the apartment opened suddenly, and a woman entered. At the sight of Leif, her eyes widened and her mouth rounded in surprise.

"Who are you? Where is my daughter?" she exclaimed. "Bella? Bella, sugar plum, answer me!"

Shocked, Leif could only stare at someone whose face he'd seen on his mother's living room wall every day growing up. A legend he was finally meeting in person.

"Mrs. Claus?"

CHAPTER
SEVENTEEN
CHRISTMAS EVE AND MORE SURPRISED THAN THE VIRGIN MARY AT BEING PREGNANT...

Leif couldn't help but stare at the woman whose legend he'd been raised on. While Santa might have been the guy everyone lauded, according to his mom, Mrs. Claus was the glue that kept them together. Mediator, mother to those in need of a listening ear and hug, a confidant and advisor, whose special Christmas cookies were said to be divine—and laced with medicinal herbs.

The woman, the wife, the mother, the legend.

And she stood in front of him. Although an ashen pallor fell over her face when he said "Mrs. Claus."

She attempted indignation. "How rude. Calling an older woman names. Did no one teach you not to mock your elders?"

Chagrin hit him for a moment. Could he be wrong? The more he looked at her, the more he couldn't be swayed. "It's you. I know it is. My mom has your picture in our living room. She used to have one in the bathroom, too, when I was just a toddler, but apparently, I couldn't do my business because I worried you might be watching."

Mrs. Claus winced. "I never understood why people did that. Who would want to look at my face every day? I much prefer images of landscapes and goats in pajamas."

Now that she no longer denied her identity, he felt justified in asking, "What are you doing here?"

"I could ask the same of you." At Mrs. Claus's crossed arms and stern expression, he almost apologized. But then again, he had every right to be in Bella's apartment. It was Mrs. Claus—

Hold on. It took him until that moment to clue in on something she'd said. Something crazy and impossible. "You called her 'daughter.' Are you Bella's mom?"

"I am, and I'm wondering why there's a strange man in her living room." She arched a brow.

"Hardly strange. She and I are—" He paused because they'd yet to define the unfolding nature of their relationship, so he stuck to a generic, "Friends. And as you might have guessed, I'm from the North Pole."

"That is not reassuring," she grumbled.

Thinking of Maurice and his plans for NextGen's elven Christmas domination, he grimaced. "Fair point. Would you accept instead my word that I'd never hurt Bella?"

Her gaze stared right through him into his soul, weighing his merit and intent. "You're telling the truth, but if that's the case, where is she? It's the middle of the night, and she's not in bed. And something happened in here. I can still sense it in the air." She waved a hand at the lingering chill.

There was no easy way of saying it. "I think Krampus took her."

Mrs. Claus swirled her hand. "Impossible. I had this place secured. Hidden. He should have never been able to find her." Her voice was low as she said, "I sent Bella a package. Where is it?"

He glanced at the table, the last place he'd seen it. "It was right there."

Mrs. Claus put a hand to her forehead and muttered, "Please tell me it wasn't opened."

"It was. But only for a moment. After the gingerbread attack—"

"Wait, what?"

He explained what had happened thus far. The first attack, how he'd taken Bella to the North Pole to gain her trust. His opening of the package, with him adding, "It's still a secret. She never peeked inside."

"Doesn't matter. Once the magical seal broke, it would have drawn him like an elf to the kitchen when cookies are baking."

An irresistible scent. "I'm not sure I understand..." His voice trailed off as Maurice's words came back to haunt him. "The old silver bell inside that package, that was one of the talismans with Santa's Magic."

"And now he's got it and Bella." The statement deflated the woman, and she sank on to a chair, head bowed.

He cleared his throat. "Um. Mrs. Claus?"

She lifted her head and eyed him with bright blue eyes. "Call me Gertrude."

"So it really is you?"

"In the flesh." Her smile barely lifted the corners of her lips. "And who are you?"

"Leif. Leif Blitzen. You knew my dad, Lars, and my mom, Bitsy."

"Ah yes. You would have been about two when I left. You've gotten big. Take after your mother."

"Where have you been?" The burning question many elves had.

She waved a hand. "Everywhere."

"Why?" he asked. Why did she leave? Why did she never return?

Mrs. Claus sighed. "We don't have time for a history lesson. I need to find Bella."

"So do I, but given I have a feeling that secrets are a large part of the reason we're in this situation, maybe it's time we cleared some up. Starting with why you helped Krampus escape."

"I didn't, but I didn't stop it either because it was time."

"Time to unleash a monster?" he exclaimed.

"You seem to have forgotten that the monster is inside my husband. A good man who had the bad luck to be infected by that parasite Krampus." Her lips twisted in disgust.

"Santa is dangerous. They had to lock him away to protect people."

"They?" Mrs. Claus laughed. "Do you really think

anyone had the power to imprison my Nikolas? The man who could enter any home he wanted through any kind of crevice? There was no prison to hold him."

"Which is why they took his magic."

"Repeat that again slowly and think about it. Who took it? Who amongst the elves, the humans, anyone, would have the strength and power to take that which belongs to Santa?"

His brows knit. "No one person, but if a bunch of magic users banded together—"

She slashed a hand. "Wrong. Not even close. It was why Krampus got away with his crimes for so long. He infected the most powerful man on Earth. No one could stop him. No one but Nikolas himself. And so he made the ultimate sacrifice."

"I don't understand."

"The Krampus infection is oddly unique in that it only afflicted my husband part of the year. The rest of the time Nikolas was lucid and aware, also horrified by what nested within. Together we searched for a cure, a way to rid the world of Krampus once and for all. Before we could find a solution, a group of elves began moving against us."

"What?"

She waved a hand. "We couldn't really blame them. Krampus is truly a horrid creature, and my poor Nikolas was devastated at the crimes it committed wearing his body. Where we had to draw the line was the elves' solution. They wanted to kill my poor Nikolas. Short-sighted thinking because Krampus would have simply jumped into a new body. And without my Nikolas to defeat him... Well, the world would be a much darker place."

"So you imprisoned him instead."

"It was the only way to save my husband. However, a problem remained. See, while Nikolas would have had the gumption to remain in that pit for the good of the world, when Krampus took over, he would have used his magic to escape. Knowing that, Nikolas rid himself of his magic, placing it inside five silver bells, which I was supposed to scatter to the corners of the world to keep them safe until such time as they were needed. He'd no sooner pressed the box holding them upon me than he exiled himself into that pit." Her voice broke. "I was there to cut the rope once he reached the bottom. I was the one to seal it with that magical grate. The one that made sure my dear sweet husband could never escape." Her voice dropped to a whisper.

So much to digest. He focused on the part that seemed most pertinent. "He gave you the magical talismans?"

"He did, and the box they were sealed in was stolen while I grieved his loss." Her lips turned down.

"By who?"

"The same elves who thought we should kill him. They decided I wasn't to be trusted with them because they worried I'd set him free. So they took the bells from me and scattered them. Before I could convince them to tell where they'd been hidden, a spell was cast. A spell of forgetfulness. The bells were lost."

"But you found them?" he interrupted.

"I found three. I wasn't in time to prevent the fourth from being used to free Nikolas. As for the fifth, it's magic was already gone."

"I can't believe this." He raked fingers through his hair. It hit him. "Bella doesn't know your real identity."

"No."

"Why not?" He whirled on Mrs. Claus with accusation in his gaze.

"Because it was the only way to keep her safe."

"Safe from who?"

"Haven't you figured it out yet?" Sorrow filled her gaze. "Her father. Santa Nikolas Claus."

CHAPTER
EIGHTEEN

WISHING SHE WERE IN BED, WEARING HER FOOTED PAJAMAS WITH THE WORDS "I'M SEXY AND I GNOME IT"...

BELLA WOKE INSIDE A ROOM OF ICE. WALLS. CEILING. She leaned over the edge of the ice bed to eyeball the floor, also ice, intricately carved to appear like interlocked stone. The detail was absolutely incredible. Also really freaking cold.

She huddled on the bed. The frame was constructed of ice, but she lay upon a strange mattress covered in a fur skin. More of the hairy blankets were heaped over her. Mostly white. Polar bear if she had to guess.

Light came from the flames burning within braziers formed of yellowed skulls holding a cloudy looking oil. For a second, she almost giggled as the phrase "Reduce, reuse, recycle" ran through her head. Not the time for mirth.

How had she gotten here?

The last she recalled she'd been in her apartment when a sack came over her head. But before that she'd seen her kidnapper. An older man, the skin of his face folded in wrinkles. Eyes of pure white eerily stared, matching his hair and beard. His horns, a dark grey and curling, jutted from his forehead. His canines slipped past his mouth. His cheeks sucked in, gaunt like his frame. He wore a red velvet robe, the kind that went over the head, a longer version really of her Oodie. Around his waist a rope was wrapped, and dangling from it were two bells that didn't make a sound when he moved.

She took in those details and barely had time to realize she looked upon Krampus before the sack covered her, her struggle lasting a brief moment—"Let me out!"— and then she was out like a light until she woke here. Here being where? Where had Krampus taken her?

Lying in bed wouldn't give her any answers. She dangled her legs over the edge, eyeing her bare feet and then the icy floor. Walking on that for any length of time, she'd lose toes for sure, but she didn't see any socks or shoes.

Think. Think.

She eyed the furry blankets on her bed. Not ideal, however, under the bottom layer, the mattress appeared covered in a more supple material. If she had to guess by what she'd seen so far, most likely seal skin. It took some grunting and tugging to pull apart a seam. Then she tried not to dwell on what she gnawed on as she started a tear that allowed her to rip a strip then another. The inside of the mattress was filled with tufts of fur. She used the jagged strips to bind her feet, winding them over and around enough times to cover her flesh. It would offer some protection. Nothing long term though, so she'd better find a way out of here.

She tiptoed to the door, each small step terrifying as she worried about sliding on the ice. Or what if bare flesh peeked out and stuck to something? Despite her trepidation, she made it with no issue and pulled at the portal, half convinced it would turn out to just be carved ice and not open at all. The other half of her figured it would be locked.

It swung easily, and she gazed upon a much larger room. The ceiling swept into arches overhead, lit by more of the bone braziers. The walls were covered in art, some of it torn as if in a fit of rage. But those that remained, even the pieces, all appeared to have a Christmas theme. Beautiful and artistic, despite the circumstances.

Within the large chamber she noted many tables made of more bone, a few carved of ice. Even a huge stone altar upon which the brownish stains gave a hint as to its purpose. The other surfaces appeared to be covered in different materials. The table closest to her held scraps of tanned skin and little pots fashioned of bone with color inside. Another table held chiseled figurines carved out of more bone.

The space reminded her of a workshop, and at its center, a hunched figure. Krampus, distinctive with the curling horns. Intent on something, it didn't seem the monster had noticed her arrival.

She glanced around, seeing other doors ringing the space. Perhaps she could sneak out while he was occupied.

Slow inch. Careful. She kept her gaze on Krampus. His arms moved, holding what appeared to be a long needle, the thread through its eye thick enough to see before it dove back into the puddle of fabric in his lap.

She paused.

Krampus was sewing? What an odd thing for him to do. Then again—she glanced at the pots of what she realized was paint and the figurines that wouldn't look out of place on a chessboard. It hit her in that moment that she wasn't just looking on Krampus, the killing monster, but the man he possessed. A toymaker named Santa Claus.

She almost took a step toward him.

Almost.

Self-preservation quickly reminded her that a kind Santa wouldn't have kidnapped and terrified her. A non-murdering Santa wouldn't have been tossed in a hole of pure ice.

There would be no negotiating or compassion. She had to escape. She'd made it to a door and put her hand on it, ready to push since it had no handle, when he spoke.

"I wouldn't go in there if I were you." The rough voice had her glancing over her shoulder.

Krampus stood, hands tucked in the sleeves of his robe, eyes on her.

"As if I'd listen to you."

"Open it then and you'll see." His casual remark, slightly lisped.

"Maybe I will," she huffed.

She shoved at the door and took a step, only to pause with a foot in the air. A long shaft blew warmly at her. No floor. Nothing but a hole.

"It's where I dispose of the things for which I truly have no use," he answered despite there being no question.

She let the door swing shut and turned to confront him. "Why have you kidnapped me?"

"You have something I want."

"If you're talking about one of my antiques, then you could have just asked." An inane comeback.

"I doubt you'd give your life willingly."

That chilled her to the marrow, and since she had no great reply, she stuck to a dumb one. "You're Krampus."

"I am." His smile would make children cry.

She tried not to tremble. "What are you going to do to me?"

"Other than the obvious? I want to make him suffer. Even when it's my time, and he's supposed to sleep, he's watching. He sees me when I'm awake. He knows when I've been bad or worse, and right now, he's pleading for me to be good for your sake."

Wait, was he implying that Santa rooted for her? Sweet, but not really helpful when faced with the monster.

"I haven't done anything to you. Why hurt me? I thought you only went after bad children." She winced, as it sounded as if she'd rather sacrifice a naughty child than herself.

"Bad children only because *he* made me. Refusing to

step aside when it was my turn. Meddling in my work. Trying to mitigate my kills."

Admitting to a split personality. She hugged herself as Krampus spoke. "That might be one of the top creepiest things to say. Like really. Creepy."

"And I've barely even started." A fanged smile went with those eerie, milky eyes. "I can't believe I found you. She had you hidden so well. I might not have ever found you if not for the bell." He fingered one at his waist. One of two. "Imagine my surprise when I went to fetch it and found you. *His* child."

Bella blinked. "Excuse me?"

The monster appeared surprised. "You don't know." His laughter raised every hair on her body. "This is even better than I could have hoped for."

"What are you talking about?"

"Who is your father?" Krampus asked.

Despite her chill, she replied, "His name was Kristopher Rinkeli. He died before I was born."

"Actually, his name was Kristopher Nikolas Kringle until his family disowned him and he became the annoying legend known as—"

"Santa Claus." She breathed the name and then sputtered, "You're lying."

"Am I?"

"My mother would have told me. Not to mention, Mrs. Claus is old, and my mom had me when she was young."

"She might have appeared that way to you, but I

assure you, she is quite elderly. Almost as old as your father."

"I don't believe you," she huffed.

"Would you like proof? Let's see what your father has to say."

In that moment, the monster in front of her changed. The horns receded, the fangs as well. The air lost that heavy foreboding. The eyes went from milky white to blue, brimming with tears.

He said only one thing. "I'm sorry. I couldn't stop him."

"Are you—?" She couldn't say it.

The man in front of her nodded.

She took a step toward him then another. "I don't understand. How is this possible?"

"You were our Christmas miracle, conceived the last night we were together before I locked myself and the monster inside me away."

"My daddy is Santa Claus?" The very idea boggled the mind.

"Yes, and because of it, you are in grave danger. You must—"

The switch back to Krampus happened abruptly, and she flinched as the very air turned ominous.

"Ah, his misery is a delight." Krampus sighed with pleasure. "And it will only get better from here. Put this on." The monster thrust fabric at her, the very thing he'd been working on, a dress, she realized.

She clutched it, at a loss. What to do? "I won't let you hurt him."

"Won't?" He grabbed her by the neck and drew her close as she gasped for breath. "Just your presence is agony for him." When the monster thrust her from him, he barked, "Put on the dress. I would have you wear the same garment as his wife did on their wedding for our special night. The white will be a nice contrast for the blood."

Realization widened her eyes in horror. "You're going to kill me?"

"Kill. Torture. Hurt. Be afraid. Very afraid." Krampus chuckled as he whispered, "No one is coming to save you, Christmas Isabella Claus."

CHAPTER
NINETEEN

LEIF IN HIS DUSTER AND MRS. CLAUS WITH A CLAP HAD JUST DELIVERED A TRUTHFUL SLAP...

Holly berries on a wreath. Leif's head filled with a buzzing noise as Mrs. Claus revealed the name of Bella's daddy.

Santa Nikolas Claus.

The big man himself.

And Leif had sex with his daughter.

I'm a dead elf. And if not dead, then most definitely on the permanently naughty list.

He'd barely had time to realize he'd be banned from the Village forever when a portal opened, dumping three of his squad: Vera Dasher, Joel Prancer, and Maven Donner. The latter grimaced. "Well, that was unpleasant, and my last time. I am flying back when we are done."

"Aw, did you get scared?" Joel taunted.

Maven offered a rude gesture. "Bite my rump. I heard the voice. I ain't taking chances."

"I'm with him." Vera took Maven's side. "There is something wrong with that space between portals."

"Did you hear the voice?" Leif asked.

Vera nodded. "And I shouldn't have. I haven't portaled in ages."

"Bah. You're all just scaredy mice," Joel retorted.

"I'm guessing you didn't hear it?" Leif asked.

"It's just a voice. No big deal." Joel blew off the danger, but the rest of them knew better. Once the voice in that nothing space noticed you, the danger became too great. Or so they assumed. Not long after, those who heard the voice and didn't heed never walked out the other side.

"You're an idiot," Maven remarked.

"Not what your girlfriend said last night." Not true of course. Joel might be pretty and popular with the ladies, but he did have a line. That line didn't involve not antagonizing his friends.

Usually, Leif would be joining in the ribald jokes, but not today. Someone he cared about was missing, so he snapped like a whip of licorice tugged with teeth. "We don't have time for this."

Joel sobered and eyed Leif. "Why are we here? Musher Blitzen didn't say much other than to get our butts here pronto."

"Um, Leif..." Vera looked past him, having noticed they weren't alone. Maven's jaw dropped. Even Joel had nothing to sputter.

Introductions weren't necessary, but Leif did them anyhow. "Yule Squad, meet Mrs. Claus. Ma'am, these are my wheel mates, Vera, Joel, and Maven." He pointed them each out in turn.

Predictably, Joel ogled Mrs. Claus. "Well fry me over a Yule log and smother me with some creamy frosting. It is her. The big lady herself."

"Big?" She arched a brow. "When did the citizens of the Pole become so rude?"

The rebuke slammed Joel's mouth shut, and he stiffened. "Sorry, ma'am."

"Understandable. I guess you're all surprised to see me in the flesh." Mrs. Claus appeared prim with her hands tucked in front of her.

"We thought you were dead," Maven blurted out, immediately blushing.

"Not dead, as you can see. More like I needed time away. The Village held too many reminders of my husband."

At the mention, much shuffling of feet occurred, as no one quite knew what to reply.

Mrs. Claus clapped her hands. "Don't be so discomfited. Not your fault he got infected. I'm actually really glad you're here. I'll need all the reindeer we can get if we're to foil Krampus."

A star-struck Maven practically knelt in worship. "How can we help you, Mrs. Claus?"

"We have to save Christmas." Not the announcement Leif expected, given Mrs. Claus's missing daughter.

"Anything you need," Maven vowed.

"Down with Krampus." A fist pump from Vera.

"I am totally down to save Christmas. Just point me in a direction, slap my rump, and tell me to go." Joel's winked reply.

As for Leif, Mrs. Claus's objective bothered. "I know Christmas is important and all, but shouldn't we be working first on saving Bella?"

"That's exactly what I mean." At Leif's confused expression, she offered a sheepish smile. "Guess now might be a good time to mention her full name is actually Christmas Isabella Kringle and not Bella Rinkeli. Given I didn't want to be found, I used my maiden name and a shortened version of her middle one."

Leif already knew about Bella, but the others? They gaped with Joel muttering, "Santa had a kid?"

Maven straightened to announce, "Worry not, Mrs. Claus. We'll find your daughter. We'll save Christmas."

Save Christmas. The words echoed in his head. Over and over.

Save. Christmas.

It hit Leif suddenly, and he blurted out, "Daphne said I had to save Christmas, but I'm beginning to think she didn't mean the holiday."

"That would be like Daphne to be tricky with her words." Mrs. Claus nodded.

"So who are we saving Christmas from?" Joel asked.

"Krampus," Leif growled. "He's kidnapped her. Who knows what that monster will do to her."

"Krampus as in Santa?" Joel asked to clarify.

Leif nodded. "He took her, and we have to get her back."

"He's her daddy, though," Vera stated. "Surely Santa wouldn't hurt his own daughter."

The hope Leif held on to dashed by Mrs. Claus. "If it

were Nikolas in charge, she'd be perfectly fine, but this close to the holiday, Krampus is too strong. Given his inherent evil, I fear what he might do."

For some reason her choice of words struck Maven, and he cleared his throat to say, "This is probably a dumb question, but why is he only strong this time of year?"

"I'm sorry, what?" Mrs. Claus blinked at him.

"So, I'm kind of a Krampus buff. I've watched all the movies and read all the books."

"Fiction." Mrs. Claus waved with a sniff.

"Yeah, mostly," Maven agreed with a shrug. "But here's the one thing a few seemed to agree on—even you, Mrs. Claus. Krampus is only around a short time. Essentially the days preceding Christmas, and then he's gone again until the next year. Right?"

"Yes. That seems to be the only time when the parasite infecting my husband is strong enough to take over," Mrs. Claus confirmed.

"A manifestation that is tied to a pretty specific frame indicates some kind of environmental factor that temporarily increases the strength of the phenomena," Maven added, showing that despite the fact he might be a lug, when it came to certain subjects, he knew his stuff.

Mrs. Claus tilted her head. "I would agree there is something about this time of year that makes Krampus strong enough to overtake my husband. Originally, when we sought a remedy to his infection, we thought the phenomena might be tied to the winter solstice. However, that usually occurs a few days before the twenty-fifth."

It was Vera who snapped her fingers. "But the winter solstice isn't the only thing that happens almost yearly around this time. According to my uncle Walter, who likes to study the planets—those in our galaxy and others—this time of year is when our dimension happens to temporarily align with another."

"Which dimension?" Mrs. Claus asked.

At that, Vera rolled her shoulders. "No idea. Uncle Walter says they don't know anything about it because no one who's gone has ever returned."

Mrs. Claus appeared pensive as she mulled aloud. "That would explain much. An entity from another dimension who is strongest when their home is aligned with ours, allowing it to take over my Nikolas."

Vera finished her thought. "When these dimensions shift away from each other, Krampus goes dormant again until the next time they intersect, around Christmas."

"I do believe you may have helped solve the origin of this monster." Mrs. Claus praised Vera.

"That's great to know and will be really helpful when it comes to getting rid of Krampus, but right now, we need to figure out where he's gone and find Bella," Leif reminded them.

Mrs. Claus sobered. "In the past, when Krampus inhabited humans, Nikolas always tracked the monster down to places the host used to feel familiar with. Their home or place of work. Once it was the host's favorite bakery."

"Krampus inhabited Santa for a few years before he

was imprisoned. What were some of his hiding spots?" Leif prodded.

"The mansion, but someone burned it down." Mrs. Claus's lips turned down, her sorrow palpable, but that didn't stop Leif.

"A witness claims they saw you there in the days before the blaze."

"Hey, don't you be accusing her!" Maven bristled.

"It's okay," Mrs. Claus soothed. "It's true. I did pay my old home visit. When I heard Krampus escaped, I thought he might go there."

"And what would you have done if you'd found him?"

"Rid my Nikolas of that parasite." Mrs. Claus took on a hard expression.

"How?"

"It's complicated, and right now we need to find Bella. You mentioned Daphne told you to save Christmas."

"She did. She's the one who sent me here and made sure I'd meet Bella."

Mrs. Claus stared at him before angling her head. "I think you did more than just meet."

The blush in his cheeks said it all.

"It appears you're as vested as me in finding her," Mrs. Claus said.

"We don't have time to waste." Leif worried about Bella's safety.

"You're right, we don't. We must talk to Daphne," Mrs. Claus declared.

The idea had merit but for one thing. "I'd rather not

waste a portal on visiting her. I heard the voice on my last trip."

Mrs. Claus wrinkled her nose. "Who said anything about portaling? I'm going to call Daphne and see what she says."

"Call her?" Leif exclaimed. "She has a phone?"

"Just because she lives in a cave doesn't mean she's not connected," Mrs. Claus chided.

"How come I never knew she did seeings by phone?" A hot huff by Leif.

"How could you not ask? Do you mean to say you visited her in person?"

He shrugged sheepishly.

Mrs. Claus laughed. "Oh, dear boy. Why would anyone visit her in person? Especially on a Wednesday, the day after seal taco Tuesday."

Why indeed.

Mrs. Claus pulled out a cellphone and dialed it. It rang twice before it was answered with a gleeful, "I just knew you'd call."

"Lovely to hear your voice again, Daphne. It's been ages since we've chatted." Indicating yet another person who knew Mrs. Claus lived but kept it secret.

"Oh, Gertie, I cannot wait until we can start having tea again. It's been so long," gushed Daphne, speaking loud enough Leif could hear.

To her credit, Mrs. Claus didn't wince. "Only if we succeed. You know what I need. Where is my husband?"

"Trapped by a monster. Who doesn't belong. But it has no home. And it can't be killed. Merely lost."

"How do you lose an evil spirit?" Leif asked.

"I already told you what to do," Daphne shouted.

Mrs. Claus held the phone away before saying softly, "He knows he's supposed to save Christmas. However, being a man, of course he needs direction. Say an address. Perhaps a clue to the location."

"It's so obvious, how could you not know?" Daphne taunted, singing the words. "He has gone home."

Mrs. Claus muttered, "Our home burned to the ground. Even the cellars are useless. I've checked."

It was Maven who cleared his throat to say, "This might sound a little crazy, but he's lived the last forty years in a pit. Maybe he found something similar."

"Not similar. The same." Mrs. Claus straightened. "Thank you, Daphne."

"You're welcome. Here's to hoping Leif doesn't make a mistake that ruins Christmas. It's the difference between tea next Tuesday and you being busy for the next while." Daphne hung up before Leif could ask anything.

A chuckling Vera said, "No pressure, Leif."

That earned her a glare.

Mrs. Claus clapped her hands for attention and eyed them all before saying, "We need to get to the South Pole, and quickly."

"I'll ask Central for a portal." Leif's hand went to his buckle.

"Wait!" Mrs. Claus stopped him. "The portal isn't safe right now, not with all of you having heard the voice. I'll go."

"Not alone." Maven puffed his chest. "I'm coming with you."

"It's too risky." She shook her head.

It was Vera who exclaimed, "We need a sleigh!"

Leif caught on to her plan. "There's only four of us." It took a team of eight to maximize their magic and speed.

Mrs. Claus snapped her fingers. "Four is enough when we don't have to carry a bag of gifts, and I do weigh less than Nikolas. He did so love his sweets."

"That doesn't solve the problem of a sleigh," Joel pointed out. "Or are we going to tie ourselves to a coffee table and give it a go?"

The fact Maven eyed it as if measuring had Leif clearing his throat. "We are not hooking up to furniture."

"No need. I have exactly what we need." Mrs. Claus marched to Bella's tree and plucked an ornament from it. A tiny red sleigh.

Joel couldn't help but snort. "Don't think that's going to work unless you're planning to shrink us."

"Follow me." Mrs. Claus ignored Joel's statement and headed for the bedroom, and the window with its fire escape. She calmly climbed out and began going up the stairs.

Not understanding the plan didn't mean Leif argued. This was Mrs. Claus after all.

"To the roof!" Maven charged ahead and clambered up the fire escape, the rattle enough to make Joel wait before he followed. Vera kept close to him, and Leif brought up the rear.

As they emerged onto the snowy rooftop, Mrs. Claus waved them away. "I'll need some room."

Leif leaned against the parapet, Vera by his side. "Think we should call this in?" his friend muttered.

"And tell them what? That we've found Mrs. Claus and are going after the daughter she had with Santa before he got put away by using a sled ornament?"

"Speaking of sled," Vera said, "whatever happened to Big Red?" The name for the original sleigh Santa used to drive before they retired it for a bigger and sleeker design.

Ding.

Ding.

A pair of bells rang, drawing their eyes. Mrs. Claus held them over the ornament that suddenly grew and grew and grew…

"Jumping ice drop on a heated skittle," Joel exclaimed.

Whereas Leif muttered, "I think we just found Big Red."

CHAPTER
TWENTY

WISHING I WAS HOME WEARING MY COMFY MOST LIKELY TO SHAKE PRESENTS SWEATER...

Bella wavered between terror and disbelief.

Krampus wanted to make her bleed.

Santa was her daddy.

What the ever-loving elf was going on?

How could her mother have kept such a secret from her? Then again, as Krampus thrust the dress he'd made at her, snarling, "Put it on," she could kind of understand. This monster wasn't her father even if he inhabited the body.

What would knowing have done for her? She'd have been some kind of messed up, because who wanted to be the child of a murderer?

"I don't want to wear your dress." She tossed it back at him. Foolish, but then again, caving in meekly wouldn't exactly do her any favors.

Krampus clutched the gown and literally trembled with rage. He raised his horned head and glared at her, huffing and puffing.

"If you won't, then I'll do it for you." Clear violent intent curved his lips into an evil smile.

She had no doubt he'd overpower her. Was it worth the battle?

When he held out the dress, she grabbed it.

"I'll put it on, but I'll do it in privacy." Stated, not asked. She whirled and stalked to the bedroom. She slid inside and to the side, back to the wall, dress clutched to her chest, breathing hard.

Would he follow?

Forced slow breaths did not calm her racing heart. The door remained shut. He wasn't following. But how long would she have?

"Get dressed." The squeaked demand had her glancing to the side and seeing a cookie had followed her in. An original-sized one, so barely as long as her hand. The icing face and buttons appeared basic in design.

"And if I don't?"

A smirk went well with the saucy, "I'll tell."

"When I escape, I am going to make it my mission to ban gingerbread cookies." She shook her fist.

"When you escape? Ha." The cookie snorted.

Kind of deflating to be dissed by baked goods. "Quiet, or I'll eat you." She'd choke it down dry if she had to.

"Go ahead." The cookie's rude gesture and thrust of his cooked dough hips rounded her mouth.

"That's disgusting."

"I know what will turn your frown upside down." The cookie spat icing from the bottom half of his body.

Gross. Like ew. Disrespected by a cookie. She ran for

it, determined to tear it apart, causing it to squeak and dive for the bed, grabbing a hanging blanket and scootching under it.

A voice boomed from outside the room, "What is taking so long? I am coming in."

"Almost done," she yelled, eyeing the mattress, looking for any moving humps. Forget the cookie. She didn't have time to make it wish it had never been baked. The last thing she wanted was Krampus helping her get dressed.

A shake of the fabric showed it would actually offer more covering for her legs than the Oodie. She tugged it off and stood shivering for a second before pulling the gown up, feet first, sliding her arms into the sleeves, and buttoning it in the front. It cinched without being too tight and was actually quite modest with a high neck, the work quite beautiful. A replica of her mother's dress he'd claimed.

But how would Krampus know that?

Had he already been in her fa—no, she wasn't ready to call him that. Had Santa been possessed by Krampus when he married her mother? Did he have access to memories? She didn't know enough about the monster. And for some reason, that seemed important.

"What is happening?" he bellowed again, a petulant child in a monster's stolen body.

"Almost done," she hollered, smoothing the skirt. The fabric of the dress proved soft and warmer than expected. It flattered her shape, and when she gazed at herself in a mirror of ice, her mind flitted to her mother. What would she want Bella to do?

Would Mom be upset if she had to kill her husband? *My daddy?*

Then again, what else could she do if it came down to her life or Krampus? She already knew the monster wouldn't listen to reason and wouldn't be swayed by empathy.

But what of Santa? Having seen a glimpse made her realize he still existed within. To kill one killed the other. A cruel fate but, at the same time, if there'd been a way to separate them, surely her mother would have tried.

Bella left the bindings on her feet, as they seemed to be doing well at cutting the sharp edge of the cold ice. She worried about her hands, but thus far, she still felt the tips of them. Perhaps the braziers kept the temperature warm enough to keep her from freezing. Yet if that were true, shouldn't this place be melting?

"I'm coming in." Krampus's patience ran out.

The threat had her moving through the door, not wanting to be caught in that tiny space with the monster.

She swept into the large chamber, catching his eye mid stride—and too close for comfort. She circled away from him, wanting to stay out of reach. "Calm your jumping hot acorns. I'm here, in the dress."

"Took you long enough," he grumbled, drawing her attention to the fact he'd changed as well. He wore classic Santa garb. Red coat trimmed in white fur. Red pants. A hat with a pompom. Black boots. He only lacked the belly and the jolly.

"Look at you, all dressed up. Going somewhere?" she asked.

"After tonight, I will travel the world and feast. Starting with you." He cast a lascivious glance over her, the kind that had him smacking his lips.

"I thought Krampus only punished the bad?"

"No, that would he my host holding me back. Meddling even when it was my turn to control the body," he grumbled, "Pity you're not as large as your sire. You'll barely make a meal. That was the thing I missed most, living in that hole. Human flesh. Do you know how boring a seafood diet can get?"

Krampus complaining of not being able to eat people smacked of monstrous entitlement. Especially since he appeared to be wanting to break his fast with her.

She needed to distract the monster. "Why kids? Why not go after the bad adults? The world has tons of those, and people most likely wouldn't have minded."

"Old meat isn't as tasty. Tough and stringy." The monster grimaced.

She winced. "That's horrible and not an excuse to eat children."

"Naughty," he insisted.

"Do not justify your actions," she snapped.

The monster recoiled. For a moment, chagrin crossed its features. Sorrow even. Short lived before a sly jab. "I can't wait to hear you scream for mercy as I bite into you."

"Are you sure you want to do that? At almost forty, I'm probably too tough to chew." A horrible comeback but she had nothing else.

"I am willing to sacrifice taste and texture to torture *him*." Krampus rubbed his hands together.

"You truly are evil."

"Thank you."

"So why Christmas? I mean, couldn't you have killed them another time of the year? Say like, September? Start of school already makes it unpleasant."

The monster slashed a hand. "No more questions."

"Why not? I mean, don't you kind of owe me? Because of you, I grew up without a father. My whole life is a lie. And how do I find out my entire existence is a sham? From you. Krampus. Murderer of children."

"You should blame the mother who lies."

"I'd rather be mad at the body-snatching, child-murdering psycho," Bella retorted rather than dwell on just how much her mother had neglected to tell her. "How long have you possessed Santa's body? Was it before or after Santa met my mom?" She didn't ask the most pertinent thing, but he answered anyhow.

"Yes, I was inside him when you were conceived. Guess that makes me your daddy, too. How's about giving me a kiss or sitting on my lap?" The leer finished off his crudity, and she gagged.

"That's crossing a line." She wagged her finger, faking bravery.

"Enough questions. It's time. Let's go" He reached out to her.

"Time for what? And where?" she asked, not reaching for the outstretched hand.

"It will be easier to open the doorway under the open sky."

"What door?" Was there some kind of facility outside?

"You'll soon see. Now that I have the power, I can finally reach the lost dimension."

"Are you leaving?"

"Not me," he muttered with a smirk. "I'm going to rid the world of *him*."

"You're going to kill Santa." She gasped in shock.

"In a sense. I will send his spirit elsewhere, and then his flesh will be mine all of the time." He wanted to end the power struggle inside.

"Doesn't sound like you need me for that."

"I don't. You're my prize for winning. Or should I say dessert?" Again, the wide, toothy grin did not help her terror.

"Monster."

His lisped words almost purred with pleasure. "Yes, yes I am."

Movement to the side caught her eye, and she turned to see a pair of elves, wearing snowy ghillie suits and holding spears. She might have been able to fight them but for the army of cookies also at their backs.

"Seriously need to ban gingerbread," she grumbled. Prodded forward, she took reluctant steps toward Krampus.

The hand that quickly shot out to grab didn't hurt.

The claws didn't so much as dimple her skin. It seemed out of character for Krampus.

She glanced at the monster—who was, in truth, a man possessed by evil—as he tugged her across the room to a door. Was Krampus entirely in control? But the more important question, if Krampus could get rid of Santa, then couldn't the inverse be true?

The door in the icy cavern led to a tunnel that finished in a shaft that extended upwards too far for her to actually see the end. This had to be that pit Leif told her about. That didn't reassure. How could anyone rescue her in the South Pole? No one even knew she was here!

The grip on her arm loosened. Probably because if she did tear free and move away from Krampus, she'd fall, because holy Suzy Snowflake, they were floating.

Or should it be called flying, given they rose rapidly, the walls of ice a dark blur? Their flight ended with them shooting out of a hole into a wintery wasteland, ice and snow as far as she could see. The sky and land below were illuminated by pink and green lights. The aurora australis, the southern version of the northern lights. Beautiful. Terrifying.

Even if she escaped Krampus, how would she find her way out of here? She'd freeze before she went far. It surprised her she'd not gone numb with the cold already. Oddly, while she could detect the chill around her, she still felt her fingers, toes, and even her nose.

"It's almost time," Krampus hissed and spread its

arms wide. "Once I've shed him, you'll be my present. Giving myself Christmas for Christmas. Ironic."

"I don't think so." Her pert and automatic reply.

"Brave words for someone who is not a fighter. I look at you and I see your fear. I also see the naughty."

Her chin lifted. "You don't get to judge me."

"Don't be so sure. I am wearing the suit," Krampus mocked.

"You're some sort of demon spirit, aren't you?" she suddenly asked.

"That is probably the closest definition. Do you know there was a time I wouldn't have understood that question. A time when I just existed. But that existence was drawn to another place where just being wasn't enough. Acting in your world requires flesh."

"You're possessing Santa," she stated as she wondered just how one would go about exorcising it without a priest.

"I am. A far cry from my initial arrival when I tried to cram myself into bugs and they exploded."

She blinked. "You can possess insects?"

"And animals. But humans proved to be the most versatile."

It struck her that, despite the lisp, he appeared to be well spoken. "How do you know our language?"

"Because of my incarceration, actually. When I first arrived, I spent time looking for bodies to inhabit. Animals allowed me the most control; however, their life spans proved limiting. Which was when I jumped to my first human and found myself pushed aside most of the time. Human consciousness isn't as easy to overcome."

"But you still managed it."

"I did. When the realities align, and my hunger grew too great, I would surge forth and feed. Making myself stronger. But before I could truly satiate my need and achieve thoughtful sentience, the annoying Saint Nikolas would ride to the rescue, wielding his weapons, vanquishing my body, and sending me to float until a new host proved handy."

"If Santa always beat you, how did you get inside him?"

Smugness hued his words. "The irritating Saint Nikolas made a mistake."

"And you moved right on in."

"Can you blame me? A chance to neutralize my nemesis? The amusing part is he invited me in. Thought rather than set me free to find a new body, he'd offer his, thinking he could control me." The lips stretched into a mocking smile. "He was wrong. And so we became bound. Bit by bit, I chiseled at him. He could control me most of the time, but in those twelve days before Christmas, even he didn't have the power to keep me out. I killed. I feasted. I grew stronger."

"You got caught."

"Which turned out to be a good thing. While there were some in the Village that would have killed me, your mother argued against it. Even *he* begged them not to because he knew it would just set me free to find a new host. So they kept the flesh alive, took away all his power.

He lost his defense against me, and I finally had a chance to learn."

"Obviously you didn't learn much, or you wouldn't be talking about feeding on me."

"You are meat. Meat is for eating." He smacked his lips.

"Cannibalism is wrong."

"According to you." He cocked his head. "Humans are a strange group. Ruled by emotions. They make you weak. It's how I managed to take over the great and mighty Santa Claus. His own trusting nature led to his betrayal."

"Who betrayed him?" Was it my mother? The monster said she'd argued to keep him alive. But if not her, who? Surely not the elves.

The monster chuckled. "I can smell your desire for vengeance. Proving my point. Emotions are a weakness. And Saint Nikolas was a fool."

"Being trusting and good and noble isn't foolish."

"And believing that is why you'll also die." The monster threw its head back and took in a deep breath before sighing, "Ah, if you could hear the things Saint Nikolas wants to do to me. The irony being if he hurts me, he hurts himself." Krampus chuckled.

"Get out of his body, demon." She made the sign of the cross. It had no effect.

"Even if I did, I'd just take another. I need flesh to act in this world. Unless you're offering yourself in his place?"

She wanted to be the type of selfless person who

would trade her life for Santa's. She hung her head. "You do realize even if you shove Santa out, you won't live for long. The moment you go on a killing spree, you'll mobilize all kinds of agencies against you. They will terminate on sight." She had no actual idea if that was true, but she was desperate.

"Maybe if I were just a simple human they would, but this body comes with benefits." Krampus lifted a bell, small and silvery, similar to the birthmark on her hip. A second bell hung at his waist.

"Whatever you're planning, someone will stop you." A brave claim to make.

"Who? No one is here. No one is coming to save you."

"Then I'll save myself."

That roused a chuckle from Krampus. "How?"

She didn't know, but her mother raised her believe in Christmas miracles. So Bella looked to the sky still flashing with color. She couldn't see the North Star. Or even the Christmas one. How was she supposed to make a wish?

"Hands behind your back," Krampus demanded. He held out a length of rope.

"No." She shook her head.

"As if you have a choice. I won't have you interrupting me while I open the doorway." He snapped his fingers. "Now or I will force you." His expression left no doubt he'd enjoy that.

Fear exploded within, as did an instinct to survive. She turned and ran. Pointless, she knew it even as she took the first lunging step. By the third, she had to kick a cookie out of her way. It soared with a "Yahoo!" Distracting enough she missed the pair grabbing for her ankle.

She fell forward and barely managed to get her hands out in time to break her fall. Her palms scraped on the hard-packed snow, crunching it slightly. Immediately, she pushed to her knees, only to find herself grabbed in hundreds of cookies' hands.

"Let me go." Bella thrashed as they hoisted her.

The cookies didn't obey her. They carried her back to Krampus and dropped her to the ground with him standing over her.

He dangled the rope from his claws. Once he tied her, she'd be done for. There would be no escape.

Before Krampus could bind her hands, its expression twisted, agonized, and from the monstrous lips whispered, "Run, my child. I can't hold him for long."

"Santa?" She breathed his name.

"Hurry." Strain was evident in the one word.

She had so much she wanted to say, but she understood she needed to flee. She had just taken a stride in a random direction when she heard a faint dinging of bells. Not the ones in Krampus's grip. They remained still.

"No." The word emerged tortured from the monster's mouth before the expression twisted.

Krampus was back in charge.

She moved, too late. A fist grabbed hold of her loose hair and yanked.

"Ow!" The pained holler erupted from her lips.

Ding. Ding. Ding.

Krampus halted his hoisting of her to snap, "What is that?"

A holiday movie aficionado, Bella knew what she wanted it to sound like. Her gaze lifted to the brilliant sky, and her mouth rounded in wonder as four reindeer pulling a sleigh appeared, their hoofs running on air. Moving fast.

Before she could bask in any semblance of hope, Krampus snarled, grabbed her around the waist, and jumped into the hole.

CHAPTER
TWENTY-ONE
HEAR THOSE SLEIGH BELLS JINGLING, KRAMPUS? THEY'RE SIGNALING YOUR DOOM.

THE YULE SQUAD—FOUR-LEGGED, RACKED, AND READY TO GO —ran fast and hard after they lifted from the rooftop, jingling as they ran. Mrs. Claus hadn't just shrunk Big Red and left it dangling on Bella's tree, she'd stashed the reins in there, too. She confided to Leif it was because, *"Daphne told me I'd find it useful one day."*

It felt weird harnessing with only four. Usually, a sled pull required a full team of eight with sometimes a ninth to guide them. Could only the four of them do it? Most likely. Would they be enough to actually gather any speed? He remained uncertain of that.

Mrs. Class didn't appear worried one bit and looked splendid in her red and white coat. She oddly seemed younger than he recalled from the living room. Maybe because she'd lost the glasses.

When they first took off, they found themselves sluggish, but then Mrs. Claus began ringing the bells she wore, one in each hand, and the chimes on their harness tingled. Power filled his limbs. And he ran. They all ran, huffing and pumping, straining to go faster and faster; more than sound, more than light, they zoomed south. They crossed North America and headed over the ocean, moving farther and farther past the equator. The world was a mere blur at their speed.

When the tempo of the bells slowed, they knew they neared their destination. The scenery around them began to take focus. Ocean gave way to snow and ice. The sky ran a gamut of colors: pinks and greens. It dazzled the snow below but didn't hide the raw edges of a hole, the plain around blasted clear and forming a five-pointed star. And in that plain of ice? A figure in bright red with noticeable horns.

Could only be Krampus and, by his side, a woman wearing a white gown.

Bella.

The moment they were spotted, Krampus snatched Bella and jumped into the hole.

She was alive, but for how long? Every second would count.

They came in at a trot, their momentum taking them several yards before they fully stopped. In moments, Leif and the others had changed back to their two-legged shapes, tangled in the original harnesses used by their ancestors.

Leif switched first, his coat blocking the cold. He shrugged out of his harness, his candy canes sliding immediately into his hands. Maven changed next, stockier of build. He wore a one-piece snowsuit and had his axe strapped to his back. Joel preferred to wield a sword. And Vera could throw daggers fast enough to take down a mega-snowbear. Three times the size of a polar and tricky because they could blend in with their environment. Uncanny camouflage had kept them from being discovered by humans.

Mrs. Claus didn't have a weapon, only her calm fortitude. She led the way to the edge of the pit, a gaping maw into the very earth itself.

"Do you have a rope stashed on board?" Joel asked. "Or are we free-jumping?"

"Jump, but you'll have to give me a hand, so I don't smush." Mrs. Claus held out her arms.

"I've got you, Mrs. Claus." The hefty Maven swung her into his arms.

It was the responsible Vera who said, "Maybe we should request some backup."

"We don't have time. We have to go now." Leif couldn't stem his impatience.

"Hold on tight," Maven declared before he stepped into the hole.

One by one they followed, Leif after Maven, keeping an eye on the glow about ten feet below him indicating his friend using his magic. Their flying allowed them to control their descent, which proved uneventful. No crevices or holes with savage creatures popping out. No flinging of fire balls or arrows. Kind of surprising, actually. The shaft itself spanned about ten feet and didn't widen at the bottom. Ten feet round, a space too small to hide Krampus or Bella. Where had they disappeared to? Had they missed a cave on the way down?

Maven activated a rune carved into his axe, and it lit. He held it aloft, illuminating the tight space crowded with the five of them. "I don't see the monster."

A statement that had Mrs. Claus cringing. They seemed to keep forgetting Krampus was also Santa. A man beloved by everyone, and especially his wife, abandoned to this hole in the ground. This narrow, cold pit. It seemed cruel.

As if reading Leif's mind, Mrs. Claus hastily defended. "Nikolas designed the prison. He wanted it to be escape proof."

"Apparently, it wasn't," Joel muttered.

"Because someone gave him one of the bells," Mrs. Claus explained. "Only with magic could he have escaped this place."

"What bells?" Joel again.

She held up her hands. "Five bells, all with pieces of his magic, scattered and hidden by elves who feared his return."

"Not hidden well," Joel sang, stating the obvious.

"I'm aware. I can't believe someone would be foolish enough to free him before I'd found a cure."

Leif couldn't help but mutter, "Sonya says you visited the jail. That you were the one who helped him escape."

"I would have if he'd asked." She glanced at Leif then the door carved in ice. "Do you know how many times I tried to help him leave? How many times I begged him to come out?"

"And what did he say?"

"What do you think?" she replied sharply as she palmed a carving on the wall. It moved, pivoting like a door. Mrs. Claus pointed to a tunnel beyond the shaft. "Through here, one at a time."

Hopefully there wasn't a trap at the end.

It was Vera, landing last of them all, who thought to question. "Were you behind the fire in the mansion?"

Mrs. Claus paused, and her face went expressionless for a moment. Before she nodded. "I didn't want him to find Bella. I kept some papers there."

Leif pushed into the tunnel, snapping, "We don't have time to grill her about the past. We have to find Bella."

He kept his canes by his side, moving swiftly through the tunnel, alert to anything. He reached a door at the far end and paused. He flexed his hands a few times, getting his grip, and then swung open the ice door. He stepped inside, moving swiftly to his left. Vera would go right. Maven and Joel would be the center, providing a shield of sorts to Mrs. Claus.

They entered a massive domed chamber filled with tables and junk. Not what he'd hoped for.

"What is this place?" Vera asked, craning to look around. "How big is this prison?"

"I don't know." Mrs. Claus finally appeared stunned. "This wasn't here when Nikolas designed his cell."

"Did he build this?" Maven breathed, looking around in awe. The intricate carving of the ice gave the impression of blocks interlocked and holding the weight of the ceiling. In reality, it held back tons of packed ice.

"My husband was always good with his hands." Mrs. Claus glanced around.

"Where did they go?" Leif asked. He counted seven doors in the room.

"Let's start with the left and work our way around." Mrs. Claus pointed.

Leif and Vera flanked the door, while the others stood a few paces away ready to lend support.

The first room held fish and seal meat, hanging from hooks. The next space appeared to be for supplies: skins, bones, even rocks. On the third, they gasped. It was a bedroom replete with a bed bearing actual blankets.

"Is this his room?" Maven whispered in a shout.

It was Vera who held up the fabric puddled on the floor. "This looks like an Oodie."

Mrs. Claus recognized it. "That's Bella's." The confirmation only tightened Leif's stomach.

The next door opened onto a pit that Joel almost fell into. Maven grabbed him and pulled him back from the edge.

Only three doors left. They found a gallery next, with images painted on seal skin and even carved into the ice, depicting the elves, the Village, Mrs. Claus. And more of Mrs. Claus. Her face was all over.

She touched one etched in the ice, the 3D artistry of it hard to deny. "Oh, Nikolas."

Her stoic grief hit Leif hard. She still loved Santa. But the monster in his body had to be stopped. Mrs. Claus had mentioned looking for a cure. Was there a way to save him from Krampus?

The second to the last door opened onto another hall that led to a forest made of ice. Towering frozen trees, their water stained to be dark in the trunk, green for the boughs and leaves. Shrubs speckled the ground, their colors more varied, golden, rusted, even a green one with red ice berries.

"What is this?" Vera whispered.

"A replica of the forest where we met," Mrs. Claus said, her voice hoarse.

They reached the edge of the ice forest to find an actual river, the water rushing through from one end of the cave to the other. On its bank, Krampus lounged on a carved boulder, fingers threaded through Bella's hair.

Her eyes widened at the sight of them. "Mom? Leif?"

The monster shook her. "Quiet."

"It speaks!" squeaked Maven.

Mrs. Claus strode forward. "The monster finally has a tongue."

"Well, if it isn't the wife he was trying to protect. I should thank you for begging for this life. So helpful." The monster grinned around teeth that would leave really big holes if they bit.

"Let her go," Mrs. Claus demanded.

"No. She's mine." The monster shook Bella, who winced but didn't cry out.

"Why would you want her when I'm the one who has what you want?" Mrs. Claus held up her hands and rang the bells on her fingers.

Krampus sprang from the ice boulder, dragging Bella, hissing, "Give me the bells."

"Give me my daughter."

"A trade?" the monster asked slyly. "Her for the bells?"

"One bell."

"Both," the monster stated.

"Is even one wise?" Vera questioned under breath to Leif.

Leif wanted to confront her for daring to suggest Bella's life wasn't worth it. But at the same time, what would that kind of magic do in the monster's hands?

Even Bella protested. "Mom. No. You can't give him anything. You know he'll lie."

"Listen to her," Vera exhorted. "If you give him those bells with Santa's magic, he'll be too powerful. We might not be able to stop him."

Mrs. Claus ducked her head. "I fear we've run out of options." Turning from them, she pulled the bells from her fingers, the rings she'd used to secure them allowing her to dangle them temptingly in front of Krampus.

"Give." The monster stretched greedy fingers.

"The bells for Bella's safety."

"Done." The monster shoved Bella forward, and she hit her knees with a pained cry.

For a second, Leif thought Mrs. Claus would renege. Her lips turned flat in reply to the monster reaching out his hand.

She had to know giving this monster Santa's magic

would be catastrophic. They had Bella far enough away to act.

Only she held up her hand and spoke before Leif could even move. "A deal is a deal." She handed over the bells.

"No." Leif wasn't the only one to exhale that word in horror. Especially since the monster threw back its head and laughed. "That was easy. Now I just need the fifth and last piece."

"There is no fifth piece," Mrs. Claus declared. "It broke and somehow was emptied. I don't know where its power went."

For some reason Krampus giggled. Terrifying and hair rising. "I'll find it. Now that I have four of the pieces, it won't be able to hide from me."

"Yield and you can return to prison," Leif offered as he stepped forward, the Yule Squad by his side.

"I am not going back." Krampus grinned.

"Then we'll have to use lethal force," Leif stated, trying to ignore the sucked-in hiss by someone.

The monster didn't seem discomfited. "You really think four of you can stop me?" A swipe of his claws rang a pair of bells and tossed Leif like a floppy doll.

He hit the ice. As did the rest of his squad.

As Leif rose to his knees, Krampus huffed, "This is going to be fun."

And painful, Leif predicted. Possibly even deadly.

A portal opened suddenly, spilling the other squads, plus some retired veterans. As they lined up behind Leif, causing Krampus to hesitate, Leif lifted his chin. "Prepare to have your candy ass handed to you."

"Ho. Ho. *Ho*." Krampus breathed, and the air turned to frost, blinding them to his location.

Jingle. The bells came from all around.

"Where is he?" Joel muttered.

"*Everywhere,*" was the whispered warning.

CHAPTER
TWENTY-TWO

MRS. CLAUS ~ WISHING SHE'D HIDDEN THE DARNED BELLS A LITTLE BETTER...

SEEING HOW THE MONSTER HAD CORRUPTED HER POOR NIKOLAS just about broke Gertrude Claus's heart. She missed her lover, her husband, her best friend. Would do anything for him, except let him kill their daughter.

Seeing Bella in danger hardened her resolve, especially since she knew her Niki would rather die than harm her. Bella was their miracle. Their Christmas baby. The only good thing to come out of Nikolas's imprisonment. Gertrude would do anything for her child, even hand over the bells with Niki's magic. She'd hoped to buy some time.

Instead, she'd armed a monster.

Bella shivered at her back as the fog around them clung to skin, doing its best to frost. "Love you." Two whispered syllables from her child that said goodbye. Oh no. This wasn't the end. Every single one of her maternal instincts ignited.

"Don't worry, sugar plum. I've got a plan." A rapidly

concocted—so many holes it could have been Swiss cheese—plan that she'd based on the assumption Krampus would try and claim the bells.

"What can I do to help?" Bella might peer anxiously at the mist, but she didn't run or cower in fear. Leif and the others of the Yule Squad formed a shield around them.

Elsewhere, the reinforcements called out to each other, but no one screamed.

Thus far, Krampus hadn't attacked.

Gertrude had kind of assumed he would. Hoped for it, actually. A bit of sparring would have wasted time. After all, if they could delay long enough, then Christmas Day would come, the dimensional alignment would end, and Krampus would weaken, hopefully enough her Nikolas could regain control. Until the following Christmas when it started all over again.

She didn't even want to think of what would happen if Krampus had gotten too strong and kept control. She knew Nikolas worried about that happening which was why he'd insisted on being locked away.

"I think he's gone," Bella declared suddenly.

She realized the ominous pressure around them had lightened. "He might just be hiding, waiting for us to make a move."

"Actually, I think she's right," Leif stated. "I'm sensing the same thing."

"Are you sensing with your head or something else?" teased Joel, causing Leif to blush despite the circumstances.

Him and Bella. Gertrude wasn't sure what to think of it, other than it might be about time Bella found someone to be her best friend. And eventually lover. Gertrude had long ago given up on her daughter ever marrying. But at least she had a furry grandchild in Big Floof.

It was Vera who said, "Why were you and Krampus outside when we arrived?"

Bella's brow furrowed. "He said something about how it would be easier to open a door that would allow him to shove Santa's spirit through and have the body for himself."

Gertrude felt a tinge of horror at the fate being reserved for her husband. She had to stop it, and that urgency finally kickstarted her brain into gear and she understood what was happening. "Bella's right. He's gone. He's using the fog as a distraction to conceal his exit."

"Meaning he's ahead of us." Leif stuck his fingers in his mouth and blew, the strident whistle silencing everyone. He bellowed commands. "All squads, form up. High alert. Head for pit rim and ice plains."

"Mistletoe already formed, heading out."

As confirmations came back in the thick mist, Maven asked, "Headed where? I can't see in any direction." The mist hung thickest around them.

"I can help with that. A moment please." Mrs. Claus waved her hand 'round and 'round, churning the air. The motion caught the threads of frost and began spinning it into a ball, first the size of a pea, that grew into a plum, then an apple. It continued to increase in size as it inhaled all the fog in the area.

Revealing the creeping danger.

Gingerbread cookies. Hundreds of them. In the boughs of the ice trees, behind the trunks. They held icicle weapons, and their icing mouths rounded as they charged. The squads, scattered through the frosty forest, went on the attack while Gertrude looked for a spot to deposit her giant ball of—

Hold on a second. With a flick, Gertrude bowled the ice boulder in the direction of the forest, demolishing trees and cookies alike. When it slowed on the other side, she strode toward it and flicked her fingers, pulling on the Earth and sending that ice boulder rolling in another direction, crushing even more cookies. She winced when it clipped a slow Mistletoe Squad member to the ground.

Joel whooped as he loped past her along the cleared path. "Go, Mrs. C!"

Disrespectful, but heartfelt.

And appreciated. A long time since she'd been on a mission with anyone. It felt good to be back.

With a clear view of the exit from this underground cavern to the next, they ran, Bella hiking her skirts to keep pace. The Yule Squad experienced logistics problems when everyone crowed in the room with the tables. They were the last group to arrive, but everyone gave way to Gertrude, many of them wide-eyed, a few dropping to a knee and many of the older ones crying. Her name was murmured on almost all their lips.

It brought unshed tears to her eyes. She'd missed

them, too. And if they could survive this night, maybe they'd be together again. But would she be a widow? It didn't look good for her husband.

Leif remained close to Gertrude in the tunnel along with the Yule Squad she'd travelled with plus a few others. It proved a tight fit in the initial pit, which was only ten feet wide. She remembered sobbing for days after she left Niki in the prison. Bereft days locked in her room, the bells he'd entrusted her with in a box on the floor. An empty container she realized once she emerged from her intense grief. Betrayed in her own home.

Was it any wonder she fled with her miracle baby?

"Bella, with me." Leif barked out orders. "Maven, you've got Mrs. Claus."

Gertrude appreciated the help. Her magic might accomplish much, but flying wasn't one of them. Funny how it affected everyone differently. Some Earth Daughters only ever got the green thumb. Elves could tinker. Reindeer from the North Pole could fly and were kind enough to help those who couldn't. Joel and Vera each took a passenger, the elder being carried out a man Gertrude well knew. Lars Blitzen. It probably meant Leif's mother was somewhere close, too.

She'd no sooner thought of the woman than Gertrude came face to face with Bitsy Blitzen.

To her credit, she didn't hit the ground when she saw Gertrude but rather summarized the situation. "Krampus is to the south of the pit. Korra and Juniper are dealing with the traitors."

"Traitors?" Leif asked, having put Bella down.

Gertrude only barely listened as she glanced for her husband. Krampus had his arms moving in a pattern, but slow as if he'd never done the movements before. And he probably hadn't. Nikolas had been smart about locking away his magic once he realized the monster was in him. Krampus never got a chance to practice. It gave her time to stop him.

"We found the missing guards from the cave-in. They're trying to keep us from getting close to Krampus," Bitsy reported.

Gertrude's gaze flicked over the combatants. Elf against elf. Terrible thing to see. But not the problem needing her intervention.

"Spread out," Leif commanded.

"Belay that order!" Gertrude quickly countered. She glanced at Leif. "I want the Yule Squad to protect Bella while I handle this."

"Ma'am?" Leif couldn't hide his confusion.

"Keep Bella safe. I've got this."

A stricken Bella stuttered, "Mom, what are you going to do?"

"Don't worry, sugar plum. I'll keep you safe. I just need to stop him before he completes the spell."

"What spell?" someone asked, but Gertrude didn't reply as she marched off.

She headed for the man she'd loved for centuries. In sickness and health, she'd promised. Not easy once the parasite latched on. They tried everything to stifle the monster at Christmas, even locking Niki in a room that should have been escape proof. But the parasite figured out how to use Niki's ability to get in and out of everywhere. They couldn't contain the leeching presence, and every year it got worse and worse. More depravity. More blood. So many bodies.

When the elves found out, they almost killed her Niki. She had to beg for his life and then spent hers looking for a way to free him. They'd tried so many ways. None of the priests they tried could purge the entity. Magic couldn't separate the parasite from her husband. They'd exhausted everything by the time Niki went to prison, and she'd long ago despaired she'd ever find a way to save him. She still had no idea what to do. Niki had been released before she'd found a solution.

The sly creature noticed her approach and paused the spell casting. "Rejoice, wife, for at last I'm free, just like you wanted."

"I want my husband."

"Feel free to join him once the doorway opens then." Krampus resumed weaving his hands in an intricate pattern she recognized as one to open a portal. While it might open here, she highly doubted it ended in the Village square.

Was the parasite opening a door to its own world? "Why don't you return to where you came from?"

"Because I like it here." The bells in his hands, two in each, rang as he thrust his arms in the air, preparing to finish the spell.

This had gone on long enough. A glance showed Bella being guarded and a slowly mustering troop of elves and reindeer, watching and waiting. It left her plenty of room to work without worrying about anyone.

Mrs. Claus sang a high note and held out her hand.

Krampus cried out as two of the bells flew from his hands. "What did you do?"

A little smug with triumph, Mrs. Claus palmed the bells and shook her finger. "Did you really think I'd let you have those bells without safeguarding them first?" The return-to-owner hex had been a rapid addition to them given the theft of the others she'd collected over the past few decades.

Those that betrayed her trust and took them in the first place had scattered them around the world. She'd found them, one by one, knowing one day they'd be important.

All but the last one, recently located. She'd hidden it in a safe place long abandoned. No one entered the Claus house in the village. Until someone did and found a bell. Someone knew to burn the candle on the dusty nightstand, layered in hexes to hide it.

Betrayed. Again. Mrs. Claus might have lost control of her magic in the moment of discovery. The mansion caught fire and burned to the ground. Not that she saw it since she'd fled with the last two bells.

Two bells that, along with her innate magic, should give her the edge over Krampus.

Judging by his laughter, the parasite didn't appear bothered to have lost half his power. The true chill came when he tossed the other two bells aside. "I don't know if it's insulting or entertaining how much you underestimated me. Did you really think I'd chance my power being stolen? Objects are fleeting. But this"—he flexed a fist—"can last forever."

"You absorbed the magic." It never even occurred to her that it would know how.

"More like returned it to its rightful place." Krampus threw back his head and exulted. "It feels good. But even better... I know now where the fifth piece is. I can sense it. It's so close."

For a moment, Gertrude thought Krampus eyeballed her, but no, his gaze went past.

She whirled and saw Bella approaching, a grim Leif by her side. Stubborn girl. Just like her father.

The monster had a higher pitch than Niki when he murmured, "To think I believed you when you claimed you had no idea where it was. Hiding it right in front of everyone. Brilliant."

The implication hit her and horrified.

No. Oh no. Bella couldn't be the fifth piece. Although, it would explain why that one bell was missing its magic. And she'd never known because the box with the five bells was stolen before she ever had a chance to examine them.

She turned a frantic gaze back on Krampus. "Leave her alone. Take me instead. I have more magic than her."

To that, Krampus laughed. "Still a martyr. Every year you offered to take his place, and every year he said no. Do you know the only reason he didn't kill himself was because he knew you'd come down here looking for him if he didn't answer and he feared I would find you instead? You're the reason he wouldn't die."

Mrs. Claus crumpled. "Oh, Nikolas. I'm so sorry. This is my fault."

"Yes it—" Before he could finish saying it, Krampus contorted. The shift proved visual, as the monster's eyes turned blue and the expression tortured. An agonized gaze fell on Gertrude. "Toss me into a one-way portal."

"I can't," she whispered.

The agonized sound that emerged from him sent Gertrude to her knees. She was still there when Bella arrived. Leif didn't stop but went charging past, his candy cane rods glowing with power as he planted himself between them and the monster.

Maven, Joel, and Vera completed the wall, along with a few others. It was Leif who stated, "Thou shalt not pass."

"Would you really kill Bella's daddy?" Krampus taunted.

"By the hair on his chinny chin chin, I won't let you harm Christmas." Joel's riposte.

"It's been a while since I've snacked on fusion elf-reindeer." The monster lunged, and Leif parried, his magic lit cane connecting. Krampus hissed in pain as the blow sizzled with magic.

The monster withdrew and eyed him with more caution. Leif waited for the next lunge, only to slip as the ground under his feet changed texture and sent him to a knee.

Maven took that chance to attack and swung with

his axe. Krampus batted him away with a punch of pure power. Then the monster turned into a slashing dervish. The flurry of blows left Leif on the defensive. Block. Parry. He huffed and slid, falling to a knee, and he might have been a goner if Maven hadn't bellowed as he attacked, drawing Krampus's attention. His squad had formed a box around the monster, but even with four against one, it didn't appear to be worried or losing.

Probably because there was no help coming. A wave of cookies and grotesque toys built of skin and bone kept the reinforcements occupied.

"Mom, we have to help them," Bella urged as Gertrude tried to think of a plan. Anything.

"We have to contain him, but I don't know how." Krampus had four of the five pieces of power, making him almost impossible to beat.

"There must be something we can do," her daughter huffed.

Gertrude could only whisper, "Pray, sugar plum, pray for a Christmas miracle."

CHAPTER
TWENTY-THREE

OH, HOLY NIGHT, THEY COULD REALLY USE SOME LUCK.

Leif struggled to keep his balance on the slippery ice, dodging when Krampus lunged. The monster moved extraordinarily fast, and Leif barely managed to block the claws from tearing off his face. He recovered and swung, but before his canes could connect, Leif's limbs seized. He wasn't alone being frozen in place.

Body framed in a magical nimbus, Krampus laughed. "That's better. Wouldn't want any of you to slim down with all that exercise. You'll make excellent snacks when I'm done."

"No!" Bella declared and drew the monster's attention.

"Don't worry. I still have plans for you, my fifth piece."

"You're not getting whatever is inside me." Bella stomped toward them, pushing away her mother's grasping hands.

"And what will you do to stop me?"

Bella pursed her lips. "I don't know, but I do know I can't stand here and let you kill everyone."

"Would you prefer I kill you first?" Krampus graciously offered.

"I'd rather no one had to die. Including my father."

"Technically, he wouldn't be dead, just bodiless, floating in nothingness where he will forget everything."

"Is that where you came from? That place between the doors?"

"Again with the questions," Krampus sighed. "And I see what you're doing. Distracting me. Thinking if we can just make it to tomorrow, I'll be tucked away again until the following year." He leered. "I'm not stupid. The only reason I haven't opened the door yet and rid myself of him is because now I am wondering if his body is the best for me. After all, you do have the fifth piece of power. And I've not worn a female body in a long time."

Leif managed to mutter a faint, "No," even as Mrs. Claus sobbed.

Bella lifted her chin. "If you try and possess me, I will fight you."

"Then maybe I should go after your paramour instead." Krampus veered to eye Leif. "Would you kill your lover? What if I infect his friends? Perhaps we can make this a game until everyone in the North Pole is gone, murdered by their loved ones and me winning in the end."

Leif didn't know what Bella intended to do until the cane was pulled from his grip. It flared bright as Bella swung it.

Krampus lifted an arm to block and hissed in pain. The more important thing was the distraction meant Leif could move, but he and his squad held still, waiting for the right moment.

Bella stood in front of the monster, taunting. "If you want me, come and get me." She even blew a raspberry at it.

He might have wondered why until he realized Mrs. Claus had snuck close, and despite the anguish on her face, she stabbed an icicle through Krampus's back, hard enough it punched right through the body.

The monster screamed and hissed in rage. But rather than whirl to attack, it remained fixated on Bella. Before anyone could react, they saw the demon spirit rising out of Santa's body, a blob of swirling red and green, pulsing and vile. It sucked free of Santa's body, which slumped to the ground.

The blob oozed in Bella's direction. Her mouth rounded in horror as she realized what would happen next.

Leif wouldn't allow it.

Despite knowing the risk, he chose to save Christmas. Leif ran for the spirit, and as he slapped his buckle, he yelled, "Portal! Now!"

For once, no one on the other side argued. A good thing because Leif soared, diving for the cloud that reached for a retreating Bella. The doorway to nowhere opened, and Leif, tangled with the demon's smoky spirit, went into it.

CHAPTER
TWENTY-FOUR

REALLY WISHING SHE COULD BE LIKE A SNOWMAN AND CHILL OUT.

ONE SECOND BELLA STARED AT A DEMONIC SPIRIT READYING TO possess her, and the next Leif tackled it and fell into a portal.

The doorway closed, and there was silence for a second before a woman screamed, "Leif! No. Not my son."

Bella whispered his name in shock. Grief. A whole array of emotions slammed into her as Leif disappeared. He was gone because he'd chosen to save her life.

"Sugar plum!" Mom's arms came around her hard and fast.

"I'm fine," she grumbled, doing her best not to cry.

"Are you sure?" Concerned hands palpated her, and Mom's eyes tracked every inch.

Nose wrinkled, Bella said, "Is it me, or have you lost like twenty years?"

Her mother moved away. "Maybe."

"More secrets, Mom? Really?" She used her anger with her mother to shove against the sorrow.

Her mother's lips turned down. "I kept trying to find the right time and words."

"I'm almost forty. Surely somewhere in that time you could have found a way to tell me Santa was my father."

"*Is* your father, sugar plum. He's not dead." Mom grabbed Bella and spun her to see a man in red and white, rising from the ground, surrounded by people holding weapons. A figure without horns, bleeding from the hole in his chest.

"What are you waiting for?" an older elf demanded as he came near, his uniform and beard sprinkled with murdered cookies. "Kill him while he's weak."

Bella didn't think; she ran. "Don't you dare!" She barreled through the circle of bodies and held out her arms in front of her father.

"Move aside. The prisoner has to be handled," the elf insisted.

"That man is my father, and he's no longer dangerous. Krampus is gone." Leif made sure of it. Her lips turned down.

"Hello, Lars. It's been a while." The deep voice came from behind her and startled the older fellow.

"It's not you. You're just trying to fool me. Not again!" Lars insisted.

"I can see why you might be leery, but I assure you, the spirit that was possessing me is gone."

"And so is my son." Lars's face crumpled, and he

turned into the embrace of a woman by his side, equally stricken.

Bella's lips trembled. "Maybe he's at the pole."

Judging by the sad faces, no one believed that.

Mom neared and held out her hands and then withdrew them, as if afraid. "Niki, is that really you?"

"My sweet silver bell, I'm so sorry for everything you went through."

"Oh, Niki!" Mom, the woman with more strength than anyone Bella knew, burst into tears before throwing herself at—

Bella didn't know what to call the man. Santa. Father. Nikolas.

The elves and reindeer had no problem. They clustered close, reaching to touch, many of them crying, and then they were singing. Not a tune she'd ever heard, the words a different language, hauntingly beautiful. Especially once Santa, her daddy, added his tenor to it. Bella could practically see the notes hanging in the air, and as it finished, stars shot across the sky.

She wished Leif could have seen it.

"Don't be sad, my child." A hand, the fingers rough with callouses, brushed the tears she'd not noticed rolling down her cheeks.

"Leif died for me."

"He's not dead. Now that he's done what he needed to do, he just needs help coming home."

She glanced at the man by her side. "How can I help him?"

"With the magic I gifted you the night you were conceived."

She wrinkled her nose. "Ugh. TMI."

The corner of his mouth lifted. "Let's just say then that you get your magic from me."

"Are you sure? Because I've never shown any aptitude for it."

"Because it had to be locked away to keep you safe. But now there's no reason to hide it." He extended his arm. "Take my hand and close your eyes. Think of Leif Blitzen and show him the way."

It sounded dumb and impractical, and yet she did it. She clutched the hand of the father she'd never known, and thought of the man she'd just met, and within her, something uncurled and tingled.

Mom gasped. "I can't believe his magic was in her the entire time. It would explain why you reminded me so much of your father, though."

Magic. She held a piece of it, and with her father guiding her, in her mind, she pictured a doorway. When she opened her eyes, it hovered two feet off the ground.

For a moment, she expected Krampus to come surging back out. More than a few people tensed and aimed their weapons.

The surface of the portal distorted as someone exited.

Leif!

Joy and surprise filled her.

But Joel said it best. "Smokin' Frosty, I think I wet my pants."

CHAPTER
TWENTY-FIVE

DECK THE HALLS WITH MEAD AND JOLLY...

Things happened quickly after Leif reappeared in the South Pole from what he'd been sure would be a one-way trip.

When he dove at the hovering spirit of Krampus, he'd not been thinking further than to save Christmas. Part of him hadn't been sure it would even work, and he'd just look stupid as he passed through the demon cloud. However, the slimy parasite clung to him as they tumbled into the space between portals.

The nothingness surrounded them immediately, which he expected, but what he didn't? The almost audible shriek of rage from Krampus. The red and green glow pulsed angrily in the space before it appeared to still, and he'd have sworn it looked at him.

Not good. Not good.

The blob fixated on Leif, who floated in nothingness. Would it be forever? Could he starve in here? More likely the voice would find and eat him first.

The voice.

Despite having no body, no larynx, nothing to shout with, Leif did his best to make some noise. While not a sound emerged, something heard.

The blob halted its advance. While he perceived no face, he'd have sworn it shifted to look elsewhere. But there was no direction in this nothing place. Nothing but impending gloom and a sudden presence.

A thought hit him. *Hungry.*

Leif had no intention of replying. But apparently, Krampus didn't know the rules for this place.

Mine. Go away. Krampus somehow spoke in the nothing.

The voice did not like what he had to say and engulfed Krampus.

No fight. No struggle. Just swallowed and then the darkness left.

The nothingness remained, and Leif feared he'd be alone forever when he would have sworn he felt her.

Bella.

How could he sense her warmth in this place?

He didn't ignore it but rather swam for it, drawn like a youngster's tongue to a metal pole in winter. The door appeared suddenly in front of him. He didn't hesitate but dove through.

He'd barely registered the cold and the ice and—

Bella threw herself at him, and he hugged her, swinging her off her feet, his face buried in her hair.

An embrace short-lived, as his mother literally wrestled Bella out of her way. "My son! You're alive!"

Whereas Lars frowned and said, "Bitsy, you might want to be careful. The boy might be carrying a passenger."

Krampus inside Leif! Bella's eyes widened, and Bitsy exclaimed, "He's not evil."

"Your son is fine. Krampus is gone," Santa declared. "And we have the very brave Leif to thank for that!"

As people cheered, Leif went for the only hero's welcome that counted by shedding his mother and scooping Bella into his arms to finish that hug.

"You came back!" she exclaimed against his ear.

"Only because I heard you calling for me."

Which led to his mother sniffing at his back. "Sure, he'll answer a practical stranger and not the woman who put up with his giant kicking feet for nine months."

"Ignore her," he whispered. "It's her way of saying she's happy."

Bella leaned back to cup his cheeks. "I'm so glad it worked."

"How did you do it?" he asked.

"It was..." She glanced back at Santa, and her lips curved as she said, "my father who showed me how to call you back. But who cares about me, are you okay?"

"Never better." Because he'd saved Christmas.

And then, as icing on the cake, Bella insisted on coddling him, which meant he got to sit in the back of Big Red with her while his mother took his spot on the team. Mom insisted on taking the lead since she was four times removed from Rudolph. No one argued.

Santa, bandaged in a mishmash of scarves, also took

a seat while a beaming Mrs. Claus handled the reins as she called them out by name.

"Now Vera, now Joel, now Maven, now Bitsy..."

The mushing cry had them flying through the air, dipping low over continents, many just waking up to a Christmas morning that none would ever know was in jeopardy all because the North Pole Alliance stopped Krampus.

Mrs. Claus took her time getting them home, ensuring they wouldn't distract the elves on present duty. Only when the West Coast and the last time zone received their gifts did she finally bring them in for a landing to much fanfare and a giant sign reading Welcome, which kind of covered everyone.

The big secret had already leaked, and as they cantered in low, they noticed everyone in the village had assembled on the edges of the runway. Waiting for them to arrive.

Waiting for Santa because they'd never lost faith.

The celebration—which covered Santa's return, Krampus's demise, the daughter of Claus, the return of the mother, and thank you to the Earth—went on for days before Leif and Bella finally managed to escape.

The time wasn't just spent on dancing, drinking, and feasting, though. Serious matters were handled, too. The elves, descendants of the original thieves, who'd conspired to free Krampus after looting the bell from the mansion—just one of many things they'd taken and fleeced with the help of some cookies—were all exiled and had their ears docked, nullifying all their magic.

Despite the outcome—aka Santa's return—their greed and self-interest had caused harm.

While Leif had regaled everyone with his less-than-epic battle with Krampus in the nothing, Santa wouldn't speak of his time in the ice pit other than to say he'd spent much of it meditating. There were plans to turn it into a museum. Bella already stated she wasn't going back.

Speaking of Bella, there was much ado made of Santa's daughter. The whole village couldn't get over the fact she existed. And Bella had a hard time with the fact her mom hid the truth about her parentage. Although she didn't completely lose it until she found out her birthday was actually December 25th and not January 7th like she'd been told.

"That's actually your father's birthday," Mrs. Claus explained.

That led to angry sex later. Leif was kind of torn about how much he'd enjoyed it.

Bella's anger didn't last long because once she had a moment to think about it, she'd understood. She and Leif spoke of it at great length. Never boring of the other's company, actually eager to spend time together, they talked about anything and everything.

They discussed how his mother was nuts—she was planning their wedding the moment they landed in the sled.

How her dad needed to eat some cookies, starting with all the ginger ones.

They even discussed a future together.

A good thing because the morning Santa, wearing a bright tropical shirt, strode into Leif's bedchamber—catching them both in bed, along with a fluffy cat that just showed up in Leif's apartment the same day they arrived—he had an answer when the big man eyed him and said, "I really hope I won't have to put you on the naughty list, Leif."

"No worries, sir. I've already asked if she'll be my wife."

EPILOGUE

ONE YEAR LATER, WEARING MATCHING SHIRTS WITH THE WORDS "ALL I WANT FOR CHRISTMAS IS YOU."

Christmas morning arrived, and they greeted it on a beach. Not Bella's idea. She liked her holidays with snow, but Dad had enough of the cold to last him a while. Especially since he and Leif had spent the weeks leading to it in isolation. It was the easiest way to prove to everyone that both men were Krampus free.

They met for breakfast on the patio, Leif's father sitting in the shade while his mom lorded it the pool, drinking early enough she'd be napping before dinner. Bella's dad was easy to spot, just look for the slim and attractive version of Santa who looked like he'd stepped out of a photo shoot. By his side, looking decades younger, her mom positively glowed. And was that another hickey on her neck?

Gross. But also good.

It seemed like everyone had gotten their happily ever after. Mom reunited with Dad. Bella got not to have both her parents but she'd also gained in-laws when she married Leif. All in all, it had been a crazy year of discovery. Love. And family.

Which had recently increased by one.

Given Bella had discovered she'd live a long while, as would her elf husband, they'd chosen to hold off on having a family. But they did adopt a stray dog that found its way to the village. They brought it home, much to Big Fluff's irritation. The playful husky liked to carry Big Fluff around in his mouth, to loud caterwauling, which he ignored. But as much as kitty pretended to hate the new dog, Bella had caught them napping together, and Floof always let Big Fluff choose which bowl to eat out of first. Just one big happy family that spent their time between her shop and the village. Flying commercial since Leif had sworn off portals.

Most everyone had stopped using them since hearing what the voice did to Krampus. Were they truly done with it?

Ever since Krampus got swallowed by whatever inhabited the portal there'd been no sign of the demon reincarnating. Not yet at any rate. But they would remain vigilant because, as Maven had theorized one night deep into some hot apple cider, indigestion and regurgitation remained possible.

To that end, Dad had been teaching her the ropes. Fighting off greedy sled robbers. Protecting the village from mega-snowbears and rampaging yetis high on ice shrooms.

But protection wasn't the only knowledge Dad passed on. She was a Claus after all, so she learned how to watch children when they slept by jumping into them via dreams. How to identify good from bad. Not that she or her dad took over the toy run from the elves. As he confided, "Letting them handle it takes a load off me and helps with my stress levels. Do you know how many times I had to backtrack for a present because I screwed up? A few children turned bad because of my mistakes."

But he also inspired children to do good.

And now that would be Bella's job, too. If she survived tea with Aunt Daphne. But she could hardly turn down seeing yeti since she'd been the one to send Leif in Bella's direction, giving her the best Christmas present of all.

Love.

And this Earth's Magic story is brought to you by a love of all things Christmas, lol. I keep thinking this world is done, but who knows at this point. I wonder how many more interesting people live in a town I think I might dub Nexus, because it seems to be a place where everything happens.

For more Eve Langlais books visit EveLanglais.com

www.ingramcontent.com/pod-product-compliance
Lightning Source LLC
LaVergne TN
LVHW031538060526
838200LV00056B/4553